The Shadow of Stonehenge

Mick Jobe

Published by Mick Jobe, 2024.

This is a work of fiction. Similarities to real people, places, or events are entirely coincidental.

THE SHADOW OF STONEHENGE

First edition. November 14, 2024.

Copyright © 2024 Mick Jobe.

ISBN: 979-8230983576

Written by Mick Jobe.

The Shadow of Stonehenge
A solstice visit to Stonehenge reveals a time-sensitive mystery.

The Edmundson Family Adventures

The Edmondson siblings aren't your average teenagers. Raised in a family that values curiosity, courage, and teamwork, they've travelled the world with their archaeologist parents, picking up unique skills and a love for adventure along the way. Now, with their parents often immersed in research, the five siblings find themselves stepping into the spotlight, uncovering secrets, solving mysteries, and facing dangers that most people wouldn't dare dream of. Whether it's cracking ancient codes, exposing high-tech conspiracies, or navigating hidden cities, the Edmondsons prove that there's no challenge too big when you work together.

Meet the Edmondson Siblings:

Emma Edmondson (17 years old)

The eldest and the natural leader, Emma is intelligent, confident, and resourceful. Her sharp mind and strong sense of responsibility make her the team's planner and strategist. She has a talent for languages, which often comes in handy during their travels. Emma has a knack for staying calm under pressure and keeping the younger siblings focused when things get tough.

Leo Edmondson (15 years old)

Leo is the tech whiz and gadget genius of the family. With a love for computers, hacking, and building devices, he's the one who can unlock digital mysteries and outsmart high-tech security systems. He's also a bit of a prankster, keeping the group's spirits high with his humour, even in the face of danger.

Sophie Edmondson (14 years old)

The adventurous free spirit, Sophie is fearless and full of energy. She's an expert at climbing, sneaking, and navigating difficult terrain, making her the group's go-to for daring stunts and physical challenges. Sophie's impulsive nature sometimes gets her into trouble, but her bravery and quick thinking often save the day.

Max Edmondson (13 years old)

Max is the bookworm and history buff of the family. Obsessed with ancient cultures and mythology, he's a walking encyclopaedia who can connect the dots in any historical puzzle. Although shy and introverted, Max's vast knowledge often provides the key to solving mysteries. He's the heart of the team, reminding everyone of the importance of family and curiosity.

Ava Edmondson (12 years old)

The youngest, Ava is small but mighty, with a talent for observation and a photographic memory. She notices the tiniest details that everyone else misses, whether it's a subtle clue or a suspicious character. Her optimism and boundless enthusiasm keep the team motivated, and her artistic skills often help in unexpected ways, like sketching clues or deciphering ancient symbols.

Series Theme and Dynamics:

The Edmondsons are bound together by their love for adventure and their belief that every mystery has a solution if you're willing to work for it. With Emma's leadership, Leo's tech skills, Sophie's daring, Max's knowledge, and Ava's keen eyes, they form an unstoppable team. Along the way, they explore exotic locations, uncover hidden truths, and learn valuable lessons about courage, teamwork, and the power of family.

The wind swept gently across the Salisbury Plain, carrying with it the murmurs of ancient whispers. Stonehenge loomed ahead, its monolithic stones casting long, eerie shadows in the pre-dawn light. The Edmondson family stood in awe among the growing crowd of solstice spectators, the air thick with excitement and reverence.

Emma, the eldest of the five siblings, couldn't help but feel a strange pull toward the stones. It was as if they were alive, guarding secrets that had long since been forgotten. Nearby, Leo adjusted his drone for aerial footage, muttering about the perfect angle, while Sophie scanned the horizon for an adventure yet to be found. Max clutched his worn notebook, scribbling observations about the ancient monument, and Ava, the youngest, was busy sketching the shadowy patterns on the ground.

But as the first rays of sunlight broke the horizon, something extraordinary happened. Shadows danced in patterns too precise to be natural, forming a design that Ava instinctively began to copy. No one else seemed to notice, their gazes fixed on the grandeur of the stones. The Edmondson siblings, however, knew better than to ignore what others missed.

It wasn't just a shadow. It was a clue.

And as the patterns took shape, Emma felt a chill race down her spine. The design wasn't random—it was a map.

Unbeknownst to them, their discovery had set an ancient puzzle in motion, one tied to a power hidden beneath Stonehenge for thousands of years. But the Edmondsons weren't the only ones watching. Lurking in the crowd were others, less interested in preserving history and more intent on exploiting it.

By the time the solstice sun reached its zenith, the Edmondson family would find themselves caught in a race against time. A race to uncover the truth. A race to protect the legacy of the stones. And a race to ensure that what was hidden would remain so—before it fell into the wrong hands.

Because some secrets were never meant to be unearthed.

Chapter 1: Solstice Shadows

The Salisbury Plain stretched endlessly before the Edmondson family as their car pulled into the gravel parking lot. The sun was still a faint glow beneath the horizon, painting the early morning sky in shades of lavender and gold. The chill of the predawn air seeped into the car as the family stepped out, backpacks slung over shoulders, their faces lit with anticipation.

Stonehenge rose in the distance, its ancient stones dark silhouettes against the coming dawn. The siblings—Emma, Leo, Sophie, Max, and Ava—stood in awe, their chatter momentarily silenced. It wasn't their first trip to an ancient site; their archaeologist parents had taken them all over the world. But Stonehenge carried a weight of mystery that even they couldn't deny.

"Finally, a place older than Dad's jokes," Leo quipped, breaking the reverent silence. He adjusted his camera bag on his shoulder, grinning at his siblings.

"Don't jinx it," Sophie shot back, bouncing on the balls of her feet. She pointed to the monument. "That looks like it's hiding a million secrets. I'm calling it now—hidden tunnels."

Emma, the eldest and ever the pragmatist, raised an eyebrow. "We're not here to find tunnels, Sophie. This isn't a treasure hunt."

"Isn't it, though?" Sophie countered with a wink.

Their parents, Dr. James and Dr. Eleanor Edmondson, led the way toward the site, their voices carrying faintly as they chatted about solstice traditions and the history of Stonehenge. The siblings followed close behind, each lost in their thoughts as they approached the iconic monument.

The plain was alive with activity. A mix of tourists, archaeologists, and solstice enthusiasts had gathered, bundled against the cool air. Some carried cameras, others held notebooks, and a few sat cross-legged on the ground, meditating in the presence of the ancient stones.

"This is... amazing," Max said softly, his eyes scanning the towering monoliths. He clutched his notebook tightly, already jotting down observations. "The alignment, the scale—it's even more incredible in person."

Ava, the youngest at twelve, hung back slightly, her sketchpad tucked under her arm. She was always quiet in moments like this, her large, observant eyes taking in every detail. As the sun began its slow ascent, she flipped open her sketchpad and started drawing.

"It's weird, though," she murmured, half to herself.

"What's weird?" Leo asked, leaning down to peek at her sketch.

Ava pointed toward the stones. "The shadows. Look at them."

The others turned to follow her gaze. The long, sharp shadows cast by the towering stones stretched across the plain, forming shapes and patterns on the ground. At first glance, it seemed natural, the kind of effect any sunrise might produce. But the more they looked, the more unsettlingly precise it seemed.

"Is it just me, or are those lines... too straight?" Sophie asked, narrowing her eyes.

"They're not just straight," Max said, flipping through his notebook. "They converge, like they're pointing somewhere."

"Probably an optical illusion," Emma said, though her voice carried a note of uncertainty. "Or maybe it's part of how Stonehenge was designed. It's supposed to align with the solstice sun, right?"

"Sure," Max replied, "but this is different. It's almost like—"

"A map," Ava finished, her pencil flying across the page. She had already sketched the stones, but now she was carefully tracing the shadows, capturing their angles and where they seemed to meet.

Emma sighed. "Let's not get ahead of ourselves. It's probably just—"

"Something awesome," Leo interrupted, already digging his drone out of his bag. "Hang on. I'll get a better view."

"No flying the drone here," Emma said sharply, grabbing his arm. "You'll get us in trouble."

Leo rolled his eyes but stuffed the drone back into his bag. "Fine. But you have to admit, this is suspicious."

Ava's pencil paused as she studied her sketch. "Suspicious... or important?"

Before they could dwell on it further, their father's voice rang out. "Kids! Don't wander off!"

The siblings exchanged glances but began making their way toward their parents, who were standing near one of the stone circles. Their mother was deep in conversation with a local historian, gesturing animatedly toward the stones.

"It's fascinating," Dr. Eleanor Edmondson was saying. "The precision of the alignment, the seasonal significance—it's no wonder this place has captivated humanity for centuries."

Dr. James Edmondson nodded in agreement. "But the question remains: was it purely ceremonial, or did it serve a practical purpose as well?"

The historian, a wiry man with salt-and-pepper hair, adjusted his glasses. "Ah, that's the debate, isn't it? There are theories about its use as an astronomical calendar, or even a place of healing."

Emma listened for a moment before glancing back at her siblings. "See? Just theories. Nothing spooky."

"Yet," Sophie whispered with a grin.

Nearby, Ava crouched down, holding her sketchpad against her knees as she added more details. The sun was climbing higher now, and the shadows were shifting, but she kept drawing, her focus unwavering.

"What are you sketching, sweetie?" their mom asked, noticing her.

"Just the shadows," Ava replied. "They look... important."

Her mother smiled warmly. "They are. The solstice sun casts light in ways that only happen this time of year. Ancient builders understood that, which is why places like this were so carefully aligned."

"Maybe there's a secret message," Sophie said, half-joking.

Their father chuckled. "Plenty of people have thought the same. But remember, sometimes what seems mysterious has a simple explanation."

Ava frowned slightly, but she didn't argue. She closed her sketchpad and stood, falling into step beside her siblings as they continued exploring the site. Still, she couldn't shake the feeling that the shadows were more than they seemed.

The morning wore on, and the crowd grew livelier as the sun rose higher. Tourists posed for photos, guides led small groups through the site, and a few enthusiasts held quiet ceremonies, their voices carrying faintly on the breeze. The Edmondsons drifted through the activity, each sibling pursuing their own interest.

Emma listened attentively to a guide's explanation of the site's history. Max pored over his notebook, cross-referencing what he saw with what he had read. Leo fiddled with his camera, snapping pictures of the stones from every angle. Sophie, true to form, wandered just far enough to make Emma nervous, her eyes scanning for anything remotely adventurous. And Ava, though she stayed close, remained preoccupied with her sketchpad, her earlier discovery lingering in her mind.

By late morning, the siblings regrouped near the center of the site. Emma looked at her watch. "We've got about an hour before we need to head back. Any final observations?"

"Other than the fact that this place is awesome?" Sophie asked. "Not really."

Max shook his head. "I've got plenty of notes, but nothing groundbreaking."

Leo shrugged. "No hidden tunnels, no ancient curses. Bit of a letdown, honestly."

Ava stayed quiet, her fingers tracing the edges of her sketchpad. She hadn't mentioned it earlier, but something about the shadows had felt... deliberate. Like they were part of a larger design. She glanced back at the stones, now bathed in bright sunlight, the shadows all but gone.

"Hey, you okay?" Emma asked, noticing her hesitation.

Ava nodded slowly. "Yeah. I just... I feel like we're missing something."

Emma smiled gently. "We're not here to solve mysteries, Ava. Sometimes it's enough to just enjoy the history."

Ava returned the smile but didn't reply. Deep down, she wasn't so sure. History, she thought, had a funny way of hiding its best secrets in plain sight.

As the family gathered their things and prepared to leave, the shadows and their strange patterns faded from immediate concern. But for Ava, they lingered in the back of her mind, etched as firmly as the lines in her sketchpad. She couldn't explain it, but she had the distinct feeling that this was only the beginning.

And she was right.

Chapter 2: The Unseen Visitor

The day after the summer solstice, the Edmondson family returned to Stonehenge. The morning crowd was thinner now, the excitement of the solstice having drawn most visitors the day before. The air was quieter, and the stones seemed to loom larger in the subdued light, as if holding their secrets a little closer.

Max was particularly eager to return. The youngest Edmondson boy had spent the previous evening poring over his notes, trying to piece together what he could about the monument's history. Yet something nagged at him—a detail he couldn't quite place. He'd read almost everything available on Stonehenge, but one thing was certain: the site still held mysteries no book could explain.

As the family moved through the stones, Max hung back, his gaze fixed on the ancient carvings etched into the weathered surface of one of the upright monoliths. Faint, almost imperceptible at first glance, the carvings were a mix of ancient symbols, scratches, and what looked like prehistoric tools or weapons. He ran his fingers over the grooves, the cool stone rough against his skin.

"Max, don't fall behind," Emma called, her tone carrying its usual note of authority. The others were further ahead, clustered near the heel stone, listening to their parents debate the site's astronomical significance.

"Just a second," Max replied, distracted.

He tilted his head, letting the sunlight catch the faint outlines of the carvings. He'd read about these before—axes, daggers, even a few abstract shapes—but something felt off. His eyes drifted to a section of the stone where the carvings seemed newer, crisper, and yet somehow... older. These lines didn't match the rest.

Frowning, Max dropped his bag and pulled out a small notebook and pencil. Kneeling in the grass, he began to sketch the patterns. The markings weren't tools or weapons like the others, but instead formed a series of intricate, looping designs. They reminded him of ancient labyrinths or star charts.

"What are you doing?" Ava's voice startled him, and he jumped slightly. She stood a few feet away, her sketchpad hugged to her chest, her head tilted curiously.

"Nothing," Max muttered, but he kept sketching.

"That doesn't look like nothing." She stepped closer, peering over his shoulder. "That's not in the guidebook."

"That's what I'm saying." Max pointed to the carvings. "Look. These patterns—they don't match anything I've seen before. The tools, the weapons—they're Neolithic, right? But this?" He gestured to the swirling designs. "This feels different. Like it's older... or newer. I can't tell."

Ava crouched beside him, her sharp eyes scanning the stone. "Maybe they're just decorative?"

Max shook his head. "No way. These weren't made to look pretty. They mean something." He flipped through his notebook, finding an earlier sketch he'd done of similar carvings from another monument. "See? Even these don't match."

Ava frowned, her fingers brushing over the designs as if she could feel their meaning. "Do you think anyone else has noticed?"

"I don't know. Maybe they wrote it off as graffiti or weathering." Max glanced around, suddenly self-conscious. The guide who had led their tour yesterday had mentioned nothing about these carvings. He wondered if they were even officially documented.

Ava tapped her sketchpad thoughtfully. "Maybe we should tell Mom and Dad."

Max hesitated. Their parents were brilliant archaeologists, but he worried they might dismiss this as just another curious but insignificant detail. After all, archaeologists dealt in evidence, and so far, all Max had was a gut feeling.

"Not yet," he said finally. "Let me figure out what this is first."

Ava nodded, her usual cheerful energy subdued by the intrigue of the moment. "Okay, but if we get in trouble for poking around too much, I'm blaming you."

Over the next hour, Max and Ava explored the area around the stone, looking for other markings that might connect to the swirling carvings. Ava sketched every detail they found, her sharp eye catching subtle patterns in the grass and on nearby stones.

It was Ava who noticed it first—a faint groove in the ground running parallel to one of the stone alignments. "Max, look at this. Doesn't it seem like... like something was dragged here?"

Max knelt beside her, examining the groove. It was shallow but unmistakable, and it led directly toward the stone they had been studying. His heart raced. Was this evidence of something being moved—or hidden?

"You're right," he said, glancing around to make sure no one was watching. "It's like there's something underneath."

The siblings stared at each other, a silent understanding passing between them. They needed to know more.

By the time they rejoined the rest of the family, Max and Ava had carefully documented everything they'd seen. Max's notebook was filled with sketches and notes, and Ava's sketchpad was bursting with detailed illustrations of the carvings and the groove.

"What have you two been up to?" Emma asked suspiciously, narrowing her eyes at their slightly dishevelled appearance.

"Just... exploring," Max replied quickly.

"Yeah," Ava added, a little too enthusiastically. "We're being curious and learning things, like Mom and Dad always say we should."

Emma crossed her arms, clearly not buying it, but before she could press further, their father called the group together.

"Time to head out!" Dr. James Edmondson announced, motioning toward the path leading back to the visitor center. "We've got another stop planned this afternoon, and we don't want to be late."

As the family made their way back, Max's thoughts were consumed by the carvings. He couldn't shake the feeling that they weren't just random markings. They were trying to tell a story—one that hadn't been told in thousands of years.

And someone, or something, had left it there for a reason.

Chapter 3: Echoes of the Past

The sun was beginning its slow descent, casting long, golden rays across the Salisbury Plain. The crowd around Stonehenge had thinned, leaving only a handful of tourists and researchers wandering the grounds. Sophie Edmondson, however, wasn't ready to leave. Her adventurous streak and insatiable curiosity had a way of pulling her toward the unexplored, and Stonehenge was brimming with possibilities.

While the rest of the family lingered near the visitor center, Sophie drifted toward the far edge of the monument. Her siblings were too preoccupied with comparing notes to notice her slipping away.

"This place must have more to it," Sophie muttered to herself, scanning the stones with a practiced eye. Over the years, she'd developed a knack for spotting the hidden—the faint seams of a concealed door, the unnatural smoothness of a trap trigger. It was a skill that often got her into trouble, but she wouldn't trade it for anything.

As she rounded one of the larger stones, she noticed a wooden barrier marked with a faded "Restricted Area" sign. Beyond it, a narrow path wound down toward what looked like an overgrown trench. Sophie smirked.

"Restricted, huh? Sounds like an invitation."

She glanced over her shoulder. No one was looking. Her heart raced as she ducked under the barrier and moved quickly down the path, the grass brushing against her legs. The trench was deeper than she expected, the air cooler and heavy with the scent of damp earth. She reached the bottom and paused, her hands resting on her hips as she surveyed her surroundings.

At first glance, it seemed unremarkable—a few scattered stones, patches of moss, and loose dirt. But then, something caught her eye: a faint outline in the ground, almost like a hatch. Sophie knelt, brushing away the dirt to reveal the edge of a large, flat stone slab. Her pulse quickened.

"This has to be something," she whispered, running her fingers along the edges of the stone. It was slightly loose, tilting ever so slightly when she pressed on one side. The more she examined it, the clearer it became—this wasn't natural. It had been placed here deliberately.

Sophie grabbed a nearby stick and wedged it into the small gap, using it as leverage to lift the slab. It took all her strength, but after a few moments, the stone shifted, revealing a dark void beneath.

A hidden passage.

She hesitated, her excitement momentarily tempered by the realization of what she'd just uncovered. The opening was just large enough to crawl through, and the darkness beyond was impenetrable. She couldn't see where it led—or if it was safe.

"Do I go back and tell them?" she muttered, glancing over her shoulder toward the barrier she'd ducked under. But she already knew the answer. Her siblings would hesitate, and Emma would probably lecture her about rules. If Sophie wanted to see what was down there, she had to do it herself.

Without another thought, she grabbed her phone, turned on the flashlight, and slid feet-first into the opening.

The passage was narrow and damp, the air cool against her skin. Sophie crawled forward cautiously, her flashlight cutting through the darkness. The walls were rough, carved from stone, and faint markings were etched into the surface. She paused to examine them, tracing her fingers over the faint lines. They were similar to the carvings Max had sketched earlier, swirling and looping in a way that felt deliberate, almost like a language.

"Definitely not natural," she murmured.

The passage sloped downward slightly, leading to a small chamber. As Sophie crawled out of the narrow tunnel, her flashlight beam revealed a circular room, no more than ten feet across. The walls were lined with ancient stones, their surfaces smooth and carefully placed. In the center of the chamber was a raised platform, covered in a layer of dust and dirt.

Sophie's breath caught. This wasn't just a passage—it was a hidden room.

She stepped carefully into the chamber, her flashlight sweeping over the walls. More carvings adorned the stones, but these were deeper and more intricate, forming a pattern that spiralled toward the center of the platform. Sophie's mind raced with possibilities. Was this a storage room? A ceremonial space? Or something else entirely?

Her foot brushed against something hard, and she crouched down to investigate. Buried beneath the dirt was a small object, smooth and cold to the touch. She brushed away the dirt to reveal what looked like a piece of polished stone, no larger than her palm. It was carved in the same swirling patterns as the walls, and as she turned it over in her hands, she noticed a faint glow emanating from its surface.

Sophie froze. This was no ordinary artifact.

Before she could examine it further, a sound echoed through the passage behind her—a faint scraping, like footsteps on stone. Her heart leapt into her throat. She scrambled to turn off her flashlight, plunging the chamber into darkness.

The sound grew louder, closer. Someone—or something—was coming.

Sophie clutched the stone piece tightly and backed toward the wall, her mind racing. Was it security? A researcher? Or worse—someone who wasn't supposed to be here at all? She pressed herself against the cold stone, willing herself to stay calm.

The footsteps stopped just outside the chamber. Sophie held her breath, her ears straining to catch any sound. A faint, flickering light illuminated the edges of the passage—a flashlight beam, moving slowly, methodically.

And then, as quickly as it had appeared, the light disappeared. The footsteps receded, fading into silence.

Sophie exhaled shakily, her grip on the carved stone tightening. Whoever it was, they hadn't come into the chamber. But they had been close—too close. She didn't dare stay any longer.

Crawling back through the narrow passage felt like an eternity. When Sophie finally emerged into the trench, the sunlight was a welcome relief. She shoved the stone slab back into place, covering the opening as best she could before scrambling up the path and ducking under the barrier.

Her siblings were waiting near the visitor center, and Emma's frown deepened as Sophie jogged toward them. "Where have you been?" she demanded. "Mom and Dad were looking for you."

"Just... exploring," Sophie said quickly, her heart still pounding. She tucked the carved stone into her jacket pocket, deciding not to mention it. Not yet.

Max's eyes narrowed. "You found something, didn't you?"

Sophie hesitated but shook her head. "Nope. Just more rocks."

Emma sighed. "You're going to get us banned from these sites one day, you know."

Sophie forced a grin, but her mind was already racing. The hidden chamber, the carvings, the strange glowing artifact—it was all connected. She didn't know how, but one thing was certain.

Stonehenge was hiding secrets, and she wasn't done uncovering them.

Chapter 4: A Hidden Message

The summer solstice sunrise at Stonehenge was unlike anything Ava had ever seen. The air was electric with anticipation, the crowd silent as the first rays of sunlight crept over the horizon. The stones seemed to glow in the golden light, casting long shadows across the grass. It was as if time itself had paused, waiting for the moment to fully arrive.

Ava, clutching her sketchpad, stood slightly apart from the rest of the family. Her siblings were absorbed in their usual ways—Emma was taking notes, Max was trying to cross-reference historical details with what he was observing, Leo was setting up his camera for a timelapse, and Sophie was probably looking for trouble.

But Ava's focus was on the shadows. Something about them had struck her as unusual from the moment she saw them yesterday. She couldn't explain it, but the shapes they cast on the ground seemed too deliberate, too precise to be random.

As the sunlight grew stronger, the shadows sharpened, stretching out like dark fingers across the plain. Ava flipped open her sketchpad and began to draw. Her pencil moved swiftly, capturing the shapes exactly as they appeared, carefully tracing the intersections and angles where the shadows overlapped.

"What are you doing?" Max asked, sidling up beside her.

Ava didn't look up. "Sketching."

Max peered at her drawing. "It's just shadows."

"No," Ava said, her voice thoughtful. "They're not just shadows. Look." She pointed to the patterns she'd outlined. "See how they line up? And here—where they cross? It's like they're forming a map."

Max frowned, his curiosity piqued. "A map to what?"

"I don't know yet," Ava replied, biting her lip. "But it's not random."

As the sun climbed higher, Ava continued sketching, her small hands working methodically over the page. The shadows shifted with the light, but Ava adjusted her drawing to reflect the changes. It was like piecing together a puzzle—one that only lasted as long as the sun was in the right position.

By the time she finished, her sketchpad was filled with crisscrossing lines and shapes, forming a complex geometric design. Max crouched beside her, studying it closely.

"This doesn't make any sense," he muttered, pulling out his notebook to compare it with his own observations. "There's nothing in the records about shadows forming patterns like this. Stonehenge is aligned with the solstices, sure, but... this is different."

"What if it's intentional?" Ava asked, her voice barely above a whisper. "Like, maybe the people who built this wanted the shadows to do this."

Max's eyes widened as the idea sank in. "That would mean they designed it to work with the sun in a way we don't understand yet."

Before either of them could say more, Emma's voice called out. "Ava! Max! Come here—Dad wants to show us something!"

Max hesitated. "Do we tell them about this?"

Ava shook her head, closing her sketchpad. "Not yet. Let's figure out what it means first."

The family spent the rest of the morning exploring the site, listening to their father's detailed explanations and their mother's enthusiastic commentary. Ava, however, stayed quiet, her thoughts focused on her drawing. She could feel the weight of her discovery pressing on her, an unspoken challenge to uncover its meaning.

By the time they returned to the visitor center, Max was just as consumed. He had snapped pictures of the shadows Ava had sketched, hoping to find a way to analyse them later.

"You think it could be a map to something underground?" he asked Ava as they lingered near the edge of the gift shop.

"Maybe," Ava replied. "Or maybe it's showing us something about the way the stones are arranged."

"What are you two whispering about?" Sophie's voice cut in, startling them.

"Nothing," Max said quickly, but Sophie's sharp eyes darted to Ava's sketchpad.

"What's that?" she asked, reaching for it.

Ava clutched it to her chest. "It's just a drawing."

"Let me see!" Sophie said, her curiosity piqued. She made a playful grab for the sketchpad, but Emma's voice interrupted them.

"Guys, come on! Stop messing around."

Reluctantly, Sophie backed off, but not before giving Ava a sly look. "Whatever you're hiding, I'll find out."

Ava sighed, but her grip on the sketchpad didn't loosen. Sophie's teasing aside, she knew this was important—too important to let slip before she understood it herself.

That evening, back at their hotel, Ava spread her sketch out on the table in their shared room. Max sat beside her, his laptop open as he tried to overlay her drawing onto aerial photos of Stonehenge he'd found online.

"I think it matches," Max said after a while, leaning closer to his screen. "See? These lines line up with the stone alignments. But these—" he pointed to a series of shapes Ava had drawn "—don't match anything visible."

"So... they're hidden?" Ava asked.

"Maybe," Max said, his voice tinged with excitement. "Or maybe they're meant to show us something we haven't found yet."

Ava looked down at her drawing, her fingers tracing the lines. "What if it's not just a map? What if it's... instructions?"

Max froze. "Instructions for what?"

Ava didn't answer. Her eyes drifted to the sketch, the faint sense of purpose behind the shadows still tugging at her mind. Whatever this was, she knew one thing for certain.

The shadows weren't just random patterns. They were meant to lead to something. And she was determined to find out what.

Chapter 5: A Warning in the Wind

The air was unusually still as the Edmondson family made their way back to the visitor center, the golden afternoon sun casting a warm glow over the Salisbury Plain. It had been a long morning of exploring Stonehenge, but none of the siblings seemed eager to leave. Their minds were spinning with theories and questions—especially Ava and Max, who kept exchanging furtive glances about the cryptic shadow map they had discovered.

As they neared the parking lot, a figure emerged from a small building near the edge of the site. An older man with a weathered face and piercing grey eyes approached, his long coat flapping lightly in the breeze. He carried a satchel slung over one shoulder, and his gait was slow but deliberate.

"Ah, Dr. Edmondson," the man called out, his voice deep and gravelly. "I was hoping I'd run into you."

Dr. James Edmondson turned with a curious expression. "Ah, Mr. Abernathy. Good to see you again." He extended a hand, which the man shook firmly. "Everyone, this is Mr. Gerald Abernathy, a local historian and expert on the folklore surrounding Stonehenge."

The siblings exchanged glances. Mr. Abernathy's presence seemed to exude a certain weight, as if he carried the stones' secrets in his very posture. His eyes swept over the family, lingering a moment longer on the children, and his expression tightened.

"You've been exploring the stones, I gather," Abernathy said, his tone more observation than question.

"Of course," Dr. Edmondson replied. "It's a remarkable site, and the solstice makes it all the more fascinating."

Abernathy nodded, but his sharp gaze flicked to Ava, who instinctively clutched her sketchpad tighter. "It's good to study the stones," he said slowly. "But you must tread carefully. There are some mysteries best left untouched."

Dr. Eleanor Edmondson raised an eyebrow. "You're not one for the curse stories, are you, Gerald? Surely, as a historian, you prefer fact over folklore."

Abernathy's lips pressed into a thin line. "Folklore often carries more truth than we realize. Especially when it comes to Stonehenge." He turned his full attention to the siblings. "You should listen to your parents and stay clear of the stones. Meddling with them has consequences."

Sophie crossed her arms, her expression sceptical. "Consequences? Like what? The stones come alive and chase us?"

Leo stifled a laugh, but Abernathy didn't smile. "Not quite. But those who disturb what lies beneath the stones often find their lives... disrupted. Strange occurrences. Bad luck. Some say madness."

"That sounds like superstition," Emma said, her tone calm but firm. "There's no scientific basis for curses."

Abernathy's eyes didn't leave hers. "Science isn't everything, young lady. There are forces in this world that defy logic. And Stonehenge is no ordinary site." His gaze drifted to Max. "Have you noticed anything unusual during your visit?"

Max hesitated, his mind flashing to Ava's shadow map and Sophie's story about the hidden passage. "Uh... not really," he said, his voice a little too quick.

Abernathy's eyes narrowed slightly, as though he could see through the lie. "Good. Keep it that way."

Dr. Edmondson tried to steer the conversation back to safer ground. "Gerald, you know we're careful in our research. The children are just curious, as they should be. Surely there's no harm in that."

Abernathy sighed, his shoulders slumping slightly. "Curiosity is a double-edged sword, James. Stonehenge is ancient, older than we fully understand. And it's not just a monument—it's a place of power. Whatever its builders intended, they left behind more than just stones.

The shadows... the alignments... they all point to something greater. Something we're not meant to uncover."

Ava felt a chill run down her spine, her fingers tightening around her sketchpad. She glanced at Max, who looked equally uneasy. Sophie, on the other hand, seemed more intrigued than frightened.

Abernathy's gaze softened, and he took a step closer to the siblings. "Listen to me," he said quietly. "I've seen what happens when people dig too deep into Stonehenge's mysteries. It never ends well. Mark my words: if you've found something—anything—walk away. Leave it alone."

Before anyone could respond, the wind picked up, tugging at Abernathy's coat and scattering loose grass across the ground. The sudden gust seemed to underscore his warning, a whispering voice that echoed across the plain. The family stood in silence, the tension hanging heavy in the air.

At last, Dr. Edmondson cleared his throat. "We appreciate your concern, Gerald. Truly. But I assure you, we'll be careful."

Abernathy studied them for a moment longer, then nodded curtly. "See that you are." He adjusted his satchel and began walking away, his figure soon swallowed by the vastness of the plain.

The walk back to the car was unusually quiet. The siblings exchanged glances but said nothing, each lost in their own thoughts. Finally, as they climbed into the car, Sophie broke the silence.

"Well, that was dramatic," she said, her voice light but tinged with nervous energy. "You think he was serious?"

"He seemed serious," Ava murmured, her eyes on her sketchpad.

Emma shrugged. "He's probably just protective of the site. People like him tend to get attached to the legends."

"Or," Max said, "he knows something we don't."

Leo, who had been unusually quiet, finally spoke up. "Do you think he was talking about, like... ghosts? Or something else?"

Dr. Eleanor Edmondson, seated in the front passenger seat, turned to face them. "Gerald's warnings are part of the folklore that surrounds Stonehenge. It's not uncommon for places with deep historical significance to have these kinds of stories. They're meant to remind us to treat them with respect."

"But he seemed more... specific," Max said. "Like he wasn't just talking about stories."

Dr. James Edmondson glanced at his son in the rearview mirror. "Folklore often stems from real events, Max. Maybe something happened here long ago that gave rise to these tales. But that doesn't mean there's a curse."

Ava leaned her head against the window, her mind swirling with thoughts. Abernathy's words had struck a chord in her, a feeling she couldn't shake. The shadows, the map, the carvings—they all felt connected, as if Stonehenge was trying to reveal something. But if Abernathy was right, what would happen if they kept digging?

As the car pulled away from the site, Ava opened her sketchpad and stared at the shadow map she had drawn. The lines and shapes seemed to shift in the dim light, as if the stone's secrets were alive.

For the first time, she wondered if they were in over their heads.

Chapter 6: The Keeper of Secrets

The Edmondsons returned to Stonehenge the next morning, their curiosity stronger than ever. Despite Gerald Abernathy's ominous warning, the mysteries of the shadows and the strange carvings gnawed at them like an unfinished puzzle. Dr. Eleanor Edmondson had arranged for a private guide to show the family a less-touristy perspective of the site, hoping it might spark new ideas for her research.

But when they arrived at the meeting point, it wasn't the cheerful guide they'd been expecting.

Standing in the shadow of the visitor center was a tall man with greying hair tied back in a loose ponytail. His weathered face was partially hidden under a wide-brimmed hat, and his piercing green eyes seemed to take in everything around him at once. He leaned on a walking stick that looked less like a hiking tool and more like something plucked from an ancient oak tree.

"Ah, the Edmondsons," the man said, his voice deep and smooth, with a lilting accent that was difficult to place. He tipped his hat slightly. "I'm Alaric. I'll be your guide today."

Dr. Edmondson frowned slightly. "You're not the guide we booked."

Alaric gave a small, knowing smile. "No, I'm not. But when I heard you were coming, I thought you might prefer someone with a... deeper understanding of the stones."

The siblings exchanged uncertain glances. Sophie, ever the bold one, stepped forward. "Deeper understanding? Like what?"

Alaric's eyes twinkled. "Like the kind you won't find in any guidebook."

The family followed Alaric out to the stones, his walking stick tapping rhythmically against the ground as he led them past the usual tourist paths. He didn't bother with the typical explanations about solstice alignments or construction theories. Instead, he spoke in cryptic phrases that seemed to raise more questions than answers.

"Stonehenge isn't just a monument," he said, pausing near one of the trilithons. "It's a message. A map. And, some say, a key."

"A key to what?" Max asked, his notebook open and pencil poised.

"To understanding what was lost," Alaric replied. He tapped his walking stick against the stone, the hollow sound echoing faintly. "This place was built not just to mark the passage of time, but to preserve knowledge. Knowledge that was never meant to be forgotten."

Ava clutched her sketchpad tightly, her earlier shadow map coming to mind. "What kind of knowledge?"

Alaric turned to her, his expression serious. "The kind that could change everything."

As the group moved deeper into the site, Alaric stopped in front of a particularly weathered stone and gestured for Max to step closer. "You've seen them, haven't you? The carvings that don't belong."

Max's eyes widened. "How do you know about that?"

Alaric's smile was faint but knowing. "The stones speak, if you know how to listen. Those carvings are older than the monument itself. They were left by those who came before."

"Before?" Max echoed. "Before the builders of Stonehenge?"

Alaric nodded. "Long before. The stones were sacred to them. They saw this place not as something to be built, but as something to be protected."

"Protected from what?" Sophie asked, her voice tinged with excitement.

Alaric's gaze darkened. "From us. From the greed and ambition that drive humans to take what they don't understand."

Emma, who had been quiet up to this point, folded her arms. "If that's true, why hasn't anyone documented these carvings or written about this 'key'?"

Alaric raised an eyebrow. "Because not everyone wants the truth revealed. And because some truths are dangerous."

His cryptic words hung in the air, the weight of them pressing down on the group. Dr. James Edmondson cleared his throat, breaking the tension. "You seem to know a lot about Stonehenge's history. Are you an archaeologist?"

Alaric chuckled, the sound low and rich. "Not in the conventional sense. Let's just say I've spent my life studying places like this. Listening to their stories. And I know when someone stumbles upon something they're not ready to understand."

His eyes flicked to Ava and Max, and Ava felt a shiver run down her spine. "You've found something, haven't you?" he asked softly.

Max hesitated, but Ava spoke up before he could answer. "Maybe. But we don't know what it means."

Alaric's expression softened. "Then tread carefully. The stones guard their secrets well, but they do not forgive those who disturb them lightly."

Before the family left the site, Alaric led them to a secluded corner near the outer circle, where he pointed to a faint, almost invisible marking etched into one of the smaller stones. "This," he said, "is what you're looking for."

The siblings crowded closer, their eyes widening as they saw the symbol—a spiral surrounded by intersecting lines. It was nearly identical to one Ava had drawn in her shadow map.

"What does it mean?" Ava asked.

"It's part of the key," Alaric said. "But the rest is scattered. Hidden. The builders ensured that no one person could hold the full truth. If you're determined to find it, you'll need to follow the clues."

"Where do we start?" Sophie asked eagerly.

Alaric stepped back, his smile enigmatic. "That, I cannot tell you. The stones reveal their secrets only when they're ready."

As the Edmondsons made their way back to the car, the weight of Alaric's words hung heavy over them. Ava kept glancing at her sketchpad, her mind racing with questions. Max was furiously jotting notes, while Sophie was practically buzzing with excitement.

"That guy was weird," Leo said finally, breaking the silence. "Cool, but weird."

"He knows something," Max said firmly. "Something no one else does."

Emma frowned. "Or he's just really good at telling stories."

Ava didn't say anything, but deep down, she felt Alaric's words resonate in a way she couldn't explain. The stones were trying to tell them something, and she wasn't about to stop listening.

Chapter 7: Ancient Alignments

Back at their hotel room that evening, the Edmondson siblings huddled around the small desk where Max had spread out his notes, Ava's sketchpad, and a series of printouts he'd managed to acquire from the visitor center earlier that day. The room was filled with a quiet tension, the weight of Alaric's words still lingering in the air.

Max adjusted his glasses and tapped the edge of Ava's shadow map. "Okay, so here's what we know. The shadows form a pattern during the solstice sunrise, and Ava's sketch shows how they intersect in ways that don't seem random."

"They look like a map," Ava said, leaning over the table. "But they're not pointing to anywhere specific."

"Not yet," Max replied. "That's what we're going to figure out."

"Any idea what Alaric meant about the 'key'?" Emma asked, arms crossed as she stood nearby.

"Not yet," Max said again, his tone distracted. He reached for one of the printouts, an aerial view of Stonehenge and its surrounding landscape. "But look at this. The alignments of the stones aren't just with the solstice sun—they also line up with major celestial events. The moonrise, equinoxes, even eclipses."

"That's not news," Leo said, sprawled on one of the beds with his laptop. "Everyone knows Stonehenge is basically a giant prehistoric calendar."

Max shook his head. "It's more than that. The patterns Ava sketched don't just align with the stones; they also match specific star configurations."

He turned his laptop screen toward them, showing a star map overlaid with Ava's drawing. The siblings leaned in closer, their expressions shifting from curiosity to awe.

"It's like a constellation," Sophie said, tracing a line with her finger. "But it doesn't match any that I know."

"Because it's not from our modern star charts," Max said. He flipped to a new slide, an ancient star map he'd downloaded from an academic database. "This is a reconstruction of the sky as it would have looked thousands of years ago. And look—Ava's map matches perfectly."

Ava's eyes widened. "So... whoever built Stonehenge was mapping the stars?"

"Exactly," Max said, his excitement growing. "But it's more than just mapping. The alignment suggests they were tracking celestial cycles in a way we didn't think they could. This symbol—" he pointed to one of the spirals Ava had drawn "—is almost identical to a pattern found in carvings at Göbekli Tepe."

"What's Göbekli Tepe?" Sophie asked, tilting her head.

"It's an archaeological site in Turkey," Max explained. "It's over 11,000 years old, older than Stonehenge, and some researchers think it might have been a ceremonial or astronomical site. The carvings there include spirals and star patterns that are eerily similar to what we're seeing here."

"So you're saying there's a connection?" Emma asked, her tone cautious.

Max nodded. "It's possible. What if the builders of Stonehenge were part of a larger network of ancient civilizations? A network that shared knowledge of the stars, alignments, and... whatever these symbols represent?"

"Like an ancient club of sky-watchers?" Leo quipped.

Sophie's eyes sparkled. "Or a secret society guarding ancient knowledge. That's so much cooler."

Emma frowned. "Let's not jump to conclusions. It's an interesting theory, Max, but we don't have enough evidence to connect Stonehenge to a civilization halfway across the world."

"But it's not just Stonehenge," Max argued. He pulled up another image, a diagram of ancient sites around the globe. "The Great

Pyramids, Machu Picchu, the Nazca Lines—all of them have astronomical alignments. What if this map isn't just about Stonehenge? What if it's part of a larger system?"

The room fell silent as the siblings absorbed the implications. Ava stared at her sketchpad, her heart pounding. The spirals and lines she'd drawn suddenly felt much larger than anything she'd imagined.

The next morning, Max and Ava couldn't wait to test their theory. Armed with a compass, Max's laptop, and Ava's sketchpad, they returned to Stonehenge, their parents and siblings trailing behind them. Alaric's warnings still hung in their minds, but the pull of discovery was too strong to ignore.

"This is where the first shadow crossed," Ava said, pointing to a spot near one of the standing stones. "It formed an angle here."

Max consulted his compass, aligning it with the direction Ava had indicated. "It's almost perfectly east. If we follow this line..."

He pulled out a map of the area and extended the trajectory. The line passed through several points before stopping near a cluster of ancient burial mounds.

"The barrows," Max said, his voice tinged with excitement. "They're directly in line with the solstice shadow. That can't be a coincidence."

"What's a barrow?" Sophie asked.

"Burial mounds," Max explained. "Neolithic ones. Some of them date back to the same time as Stonehenge."

Ava's grip on her sketchpad tightened. "So... the shadows are pointing to them?"

"Maybe," Max said. "Or maybe they're pointing beyond them."

The family hiked out to the barrows, the soft grass crunching beneath their feet. The mounds were modest compared to Stonehenge, their rounded shapes blending almost seamlessly with the landscape. Yet there was an undeniable sense of significance, as if the ground itself was holding its breath.

Max crouched near one of the mounds, studying the layout. "Look at this. The alignment continues past the barrows, heading toward... there." He pointed to a distant hill where a small cluster of standing stones was barely visible.

"What's that?" Emma asked, shading her eyes.

"The Cursus," their father answered, stepping closer. "It's a massive earthwork near Stonehenge. Some believe it was part of a ceremonial route, but no one really knows what it was used for."

Ava flipped through her sketchpad, her pencil moving quickly. "What if it's connected? The shadows, the stars, the spirals... what if it's all part of the same system?"

Max nodded. "If we can trace the alignments further, we might be able to figure out what they were trying to preserve."

As the sun began to dip below the horizon, the siblings stood on the hill, gazing out at the landscape that stretched before them. For the first time, Stonehenge didn't feel like an isolated monument. It felt like a piece of something much larger—a puzzle that spanned centuries and continents.

Max turned to Ava, his voice quiet. "This isn't just about Stonehenge anymore. This is about something bigger."

Ava didn't reply, but in her heart, she knew he was right. The map in her sketchpad wasn't just a clue—it was an invitation. And they were only beginning to understand what it meant.

Chapter 8: Tech and Time

The midday sun blazed down on the Salisbury Plain as the Edmondson siblings stood in the shadow of Stonehenge. While Max and Ava busied themselves with their maps and alignments, Leo crouched nearby, tinkering with his drone. His hands moved deftly, calibrating the camera and double-checking the GPS settings.

"Why do you need the drone for this?" Emma asked, crossing her arms as she watched him work. "We've already got maps."

Leo looked up with a grin. "Maps show you what people already know. The drone shows you what they missed."

Emma raised an eyebrow, unconvinced. "Like what?"

"Like patterns in the landscape," Leo explained. "Crop marks, soil disturbances—stuff you can't see from the ground but jumps out when you're in the air."

Max perked up from where he was studying Ava's sketchpad. "That's actually smart. Aerial views can reveal traces of ancient structures, even ones that have been buried for centuries."

"Thank you," Leo said, shooting Emma a smug look as he launched the drone into the air. It buzzed to life, rising steadily above the stones before darting off toward the open fields beyond.

"Just don't get us in trouble," Emma warned. "You know they're strict about flying drones near heritage sites."

Leo waved her off, his eyes glued to the tablet in his hands as the drone's live feed appeared on the screen. The camera panned across the rolling green fields, capturing the sweeping beauty of the plain. At first, it seemed unremarkable—a patchwork of grass and dirt paths stretching into the distance.

But then, something caught Leo's eye.

"Wait a second," he muttered, zooming in on the feed. The drone hovered over a section of the plain where the grass seemed slightly darker in long, curving lines.

"What is it?" Ava asked, peering over his shoulder.

"Look." Leo adjusted the tablet, pointing to the screen. "See those lines? They're too regular to be natural."

Max leaned in, his face lighting up. "Those could be crop marks. When ancient structures like ditches or walls are buried, they affect how plants grow above them. That's why you get patterns like this."

"Exactly," Leo said, steering the drone lower for a closer view. The lines formed a series of concentric circles, faint but unmistakable, radiating outward like ripples in a pond.

"It's like a mirror of Stonehenge," Ava said softly, her eyes wide. "But it's underground."

"Or what's left of it," Max added. "This could be another monument that's been buried or destroyed over time."

Emma frowned, stepping closer to the group. "Why hasn't anyone noticed this before?"

"Because it's subtle," Leo replied. "You'd only see it from above, and only under the right conditions. The angle of the sun, the time of year—it all matters."

Sophie, who had been unusually quiet, smirked. "So you're saying your little toy just found something archaeologists missed?"

"Looks like it," Leo said with a grin, steering the drone further along the pattern. The circles seemed to converge at a central point, where the grass was particularly thin, almost barren.

"What's that?" Ava asked, pointing to the screen.

Leo maneuvered the drone closer to the center, where a faint rectangular outline was just visible. The edges were sharp and precise, contrasting with the natural curves of the surrounding landscape.

"That's not natural," Max said, his voice tinged with excitement. "It's a foundation. Or a doorway."

"A doorway to what?" Sophie asked, her tone laced with intrigue.

"We won't know until we check it out," Leo said, already bringing the drone back toward their location.

Minutes later, the siblings stood in the field, their boots sinking slightly into the soft grass. Leo had marked the central point on the drone's GPS, and they quickly found the patch of thin grass where the rectangular shape had been visible.

"It's right here," Leo said, his voice buzzing with energy. "Whatever it is, it's directly below us."

Max crouched down, running his fingers over the ground. "The soil feels compacted, like something heavy was here. But it's too buried to see anything from the surface."

"Maybe it's an entrance," Ava suggested, clutching her sketchpad. "Like the passage Sophie found."

Sophie's eyes lit up. "Should we start digging?"

Emma rolled her eyes. "We can't just dig up a protected site, Sophie. There are rules."

"That's boring," Sophie muttered, kicking at the dirt with the toe of her boot.

Leo stood back, studying the area. "We don't need to dig. If there's anything under here, I can scan it."

"How?" Emma asked.

"With this." Leo pulled a small handheld device from his bag—a ground-penetrating radar unit he'd modified himself. "It's not as powerful as the ones archaeologists use, but it'll give us a rough idea of what's below the surface."

"Why do you even have that?" Emma asked, exasperated.

"Because I'm awesome," Leo replied, already setting up the device.

The siblings watched as he slowly swept the radar over the area, the screen lighting up with faint, blocky shapes beneath the ground. The rectangular outline was clearly visible, along with what appeared to be a series of smaller, circular structures surrounding it.

"It's a building," Max said, his voice filled with wonder. "An ancient one."

"But why is it here?" Ava asked. "And why is it connected to the shadows and the map?"

"That's what we're going to find out," Leo said, his grin widening. "Whatever this is, it's big. And I don't think anyone else knows it's here."

As they packed up their gear and prepared to return to the visitor center, the siblings couldn't stop talking about their discovery. The hidden patterns in the field felt like a revelation, a glimpse into a part of Stonehenge's history that had been lost to time.

But as they walked away, a chill breeze swept across the plain, carrying with it a faint whisper—so soft and fleeting that none of them were sure if they'd imagined it.

Ava glanced over her shoulder, her heart racing. She couldn't shake the feeling that the ground beneath their feet wasn't just holding secrets.

It was watching them.

Chapter 9: Dangerous Curiosity

The afternoon sun cast a warm, golden light across the Salisbury Plain, but Sophie Edmondson felt a different kind of heat as she stood near the restricted area she'd explored just days before. Her heart pounded with excitement as she stared at the slab of stone she'd uncovered. She had told no one about what lay beneath—not even her siblings. The idea of returning alone had been too tempting to resist.

"I'll just take another look," she muttered to herself, crouching down and brushing her hand over the faint edges of the stone slab. "No big deal."

The passage she'd found last time seemed too deliberate, too important to leave unexplored. Armed with a flashlight, a small multi-tool from Leo's gear stash, and her growing sense of adventure, Sophie wedged the tool into the gap and pushed with all her strength. The slab shifted slightly, enough for her to crawl through once more.

The moment she slid into the passage, the air turned cooler and heavier, filled with the scent of damp earth and ancient stone. Sophie flicked on her flashlight, the beam cutting through the darkness as she carefully navigated the narrow tunnel.

The hidden chamber looked exactly as she'd left it—small, circular, and quiet, with its central platform still coated in a thin layer of dust. Sophie stepped cautiously into the space, her flashlight illuminating the strange carvings on the walls. Swirls, spirals, and geometric patterns stared back at her, as if the stones themselves were alive.

"Okay," she whispered, aiming her flashlight at the platform. "Let's see if there's anything I missed."

Her fingers brushed over the carvings, feeling the grooves and ridges that formed the designs. She ran her light across the walls, looking for anything unusual. As her beam passed over one section, she noticed a small indentation near the floor—an out-of-place crack that seemed too precise to be a natural flaw.

"What are you hiding?" she murmured, crouching down to inspect it.

Sophie reached out to touch the crack, pressing lightly on the edges. For a moment, nothing happened. Then, with a faint click, the floor beneath her shifted slightly, dropping by less than an inch. A sudden, low rumble filled the chamber.

Her heart leapt into her throat. "That can't be good."

Before she could move, a sharp grinding noise echoed through the space, and the central platform began to lower into the floor, revealing a deep pit lined with jagged stones. Dust and small rocks tumbled into the dark void as the rumbling grew louder.

Sophie scrambled backward, her flashlight shaking in her hand. The edges of the pit were crumbling, threatening to pull more of the floor into its depths. She tried to steady herself, but her foot slipped on the uneven surface, and she fell hard onto her hands and knees.

"Okay, Sophie," she muttered, her voice trembling. "Don't panic. Just—get—out!"

She scrambled to her feet, but as she turned toward the tunnel, a section of the wall began to shift. Stones slid inward, revealing a series of jagged spikes that protruded from hidden recesses. It was like something out of a movie—a trap designed to prevent anyone from escaping once triggered.

Her pulse raced. "Are you kidding me?"

The ground beneath her was still trembling, and the pit in the center of the chamber was growing wider. Sophie scanned the room desperately, searching for a way out. Her flashlight beam landed on a narrow ledge running along the wall, just wide enough for her to balance on.

"Better than nothing," she said, steeling herself.

She climbed onto the ledge, her hands pressed against the cold stone for balance. The spikes continued to extend toward her, forcing her to inch along the narrow path with growing urgency. Every step sent pebbles skittering into the void below, the sound echoing ominously in the chamber.

Halfway around the ledge, her foot slipped. Sophie gasped, her arms flailing for balance as her flashlight clattered into the pit. Darkness closed in, the faint glow from the tunnel entrance her only source of light.

"Great," she muttered, her voice shaking. "This is fine. Totally fine."

Gritting her teeth, she pressed forward, one careful step at a time. Her heart thundered in her chest as the rumbling subsided slightly, the trap mechanisms settling into place. The pit, however, remained open, its jagged edges a stark reminder of what waited below.

When she finally reached the tunnel entrance, Sophie nearly collapsed with relief. She pulled herself into the narrow passage, her palms scraped and her knees trembling. Crawling as fast as she could, she emerged into the open air, the sunlight blinding after the darkness of the chamber.

She rolled onto her back, gasping for breath as she stared up at the clear sky. Her clothes were covered in dirt, her hands trembling from the adrenaline still coursing through her veins.

"That," she said aloud, her voice shaking, "was not worth it."

But even as she lay there, catching her breath, she couldn't stop her mind from racing. The trap she had triggered wasn't just a defence—it was a warning. Whatever was hidden beneath Stonehenge was meant to stay hidden.

The question now wasn't just how she would explain this to her siblings. It was whether they were ready to face whatever secrets the stones were guarding.

Chapter 10: The Language of Shadows

The Edmondson siblings gathered around the small desk in their hotel room that night, the tension in the air thick with unanswered questions. Sophie's harrowing story about the hidden chamber and its deadly trap had left them shaken but also more determined than ever to understand the secrets of Stonehenge. The sketchpad, Leo's drone footage, and Max's notes lay scattered across the desk, a chaotic collection of clues waiting to be pieced together.

Emma sat in the center of the storm, her sharp eyes scanning the drawings and notes with intense focus. She had been quiet during Sophie's recounting, but now her mind was racing, piecing together fragments of information that had been gnawing at her since the solstice.

"Let's start with what we know," Emma said, her voice steady. "The shadows during the solstice created a map. Ava sketched it, and Max identified the alignments with celestial patterns. Sophie found a hidden chamber tied to those same patterns. Everything points to Stonehenge being more than just a monument."

"So, what is it?" Leo asked, leaning back in his chair. "An ancient star calendar? A ceremonial site?"

"Maybe both," Max said, but Emma shook her head.

"It's something bigger," she said, pointing to Ava's sketchpad. "Look at the symbols in the shadows. They're not just random designs—they're deliberate, like a language."

"A language?" Sophie echoed, still nursing a scrape on her arm from her earlier adventure. "Do you think someone could actually read them?"

"That's what I'm trying to figure out," Emma replied. She grabbed one of Max's books, flipping through pages of ancient symbols and inscriptions from sites around the world. "These spirals and intersecting lines—they remind me of carvings found at other

Neolithic sites. They're not words, but they're not just decorative either. They're a way of conveying information."

"Like a code," Ava said, her voice quiet but thoughtful.

Emma nodded. "Exactly."

Over the next hour, the room was filled with the sound of pages turning, pens scratching, and occasional murmurs of discovery. Emma worked methodically, comparing Ava's sketches to Max's books and the images Leo had captured with his drone. Slowly, a pattern began to emerge.

"These symbols here," Emma said, pointing to a set of spirals in Ava's sketch, "are almost identical to ones found at Newgrange in Ireland. That site is also aligned with the solstices. And here—" she tapped another section "—this spiral matches carvings found at Skara Brae in Scotland. Both sites are linked to early astronomical knowledge."

"So Stonehenge is connected to other sites?" Max asked, his brow furrowed.

"It looks that way," Emma replied. "But it's not just about the alignments. There's something else."

She flipped open a fresh page in her notebook, drawing the symbols Ava had captured in the shadows. Her pencil moved quickly as she connected the spirals and lines into a larger pattern, one that began to resemble a key.

"This isn't just a map or a calendar," Emma said, her voice filled with quiet certainty. "It's a set of instructions."

"Instructions for what?" Sophie asked, leaning forward.

Emma's pencil stilled. "For finding something. A long-lost artifact, maybe. Something the builders of Stonehenge thought was important enough to hide."

"An artifact?" Leo asked, his eyes widening. "Like what?"

Emma sighed. "I don't know exactly. But these symbols—" she gestured to the interconnected spirals "—suggest it's tied to time. The spirals represent cycles: of the sun, the stars, and maybe even something more abstract."

"Like a timekeeper?" Ava suggested, her eyes lighting up.

"Possibly," Emma said. "Or a device meant to measure time in ways we can't even imagine."

The siblings fell silent, the weight of Emma's words settling over them. Stonehenge had always been a place of mystery, but the idea that it might hold a key to something as profound as time itself was staggering.

"If this artifact is so important," Max said carefully, "then why hasn't anyone found it?"

"Because they didn't know where to look," Emma said. "The symbols are the key, but they're only visible during the solstice. And even then, you'd need to know how to interpret them."

"Which we do now," Sophie said with a grin. "So, where does it lead?"

Emma glanced at Ava's sketchpad, then at the drone footage. "The central shadow on Ava's map points toward the Cursus. But based on what I've pieced together, I think that's just a waypoint. The real destination is farther out—possibly underground."

"Another hidden chamber?" Leo asked, raising an eyebrow.

"Maybe," Emma replied. "But we need more information. The symbols suggest there's more than one clue. If we can decipher the rest of the map, we might be able to pinpoint the exact location."

As the siblings worked late into the night, the pieces of the puzzle began to fall into place. Emma's methodical approach had transformed the chaotic collection of notes and sketches into a coherent theory, one that pointed to a hidden purpose behind Stonehenge's design.

But as they prepared to test their ideas the next day, Emma couldn't shake the feeling that they weren't the only ones following the trail. Alaric's cryptic warnings, Abernathy's ominous words about the curse of the stones, and Sophie's close call all hinted at dangers they had yet to face.

And if Stonehenge's builders had gone to such lengths to hide the artifact, Emma wondered, what were they trying to protect it from?

Chapter 11: A Forgotten Code

The Edmondson siblings were gathered in their hotel room once again, the table covered in an organized chaos of papers, notebooks, and printouts. Emma had laid out Ava's shadow map, Max's historical notes, and the drone footage Leo had captured. Sophie had even brought in her sketch of the chamber she'd found, its symbols now serving as a new piece of the puzzle. The room buzzed with the energy of a group on the verge of a breakthrough.

"We're missing something," Emma said, pacing back and forth. Her eyes flicked between the materials on the table. "These symbols keep showing up—on Ava's sketch, in the chamber Sophie found, and even in the carvings Max documented. They're connected, but we're not seeing the bigger picture."

"Maybe we're looking at it wrong," Max said, flipping through one of his books. "These spirals and lines—they're part of ancient symbolic systems, but they also show patterns. If Stonehenge is a map, what if it's also a sequence? Like steps you have to follow?"

"A sequence for what?" Leo asked, spinning a pen between his fingers.

"To unlock the artifact," Ava said, her voice quiet but certain. She was sitting cross-legged on the floor, her sketchpad resting in her lap. "The spirals on my map—they're not just shapes. They're pointing to something."

Sophie leaned forward, resting her elbows on the table. "Okay, so how do we figure out the sequence? We've got a bunch of drawings, some carvings, and Max's history lessons. What's the next step?"

Emma sighed, rubbing her temples. "We need to crack the symbols. If we can understand their order, we might be able to follow them to the next clue."

Max spread a series of images across the table—close-ups of carvings from Stonehenge, drone images of the hidden patterns in the field, and symbols from Sophie's chamber sketch. "Let's start with the basics," he said, pointing to a repeated symbol: a spiral surrounded by intersecting lines. "This one shows up everywhere. It's clearly important."

"I think it represents the solstice," Ava said, flipping through her sketchpad. "Look at how it matches the way the shadows align. It's like a marker."

"But a marker for what?" Sophie asked.

"Maybe it's telling us where to start," Max said. "If we treat the spiral as the beginning of the sequence, then the lines around it could be instructions for what comes next."

Emma nodded, her eyes lighting up. "What if it's not just a map? What if it's a path?"

"A path to where?" Leo asked.

"That's what we're going to figure out," Emma replied, her confidence growing. She grabbed a blank sheet of paper and began to draw. "Let's put the symbols in order based on where they show up on Ava's map, the drone footage, and the chamber."

The siblings worked late into the night, piecing together the sequence like a massive jigsaw puzzle. Ava sketched connections between symbols, Max cross-referenced historical records, and Leo used his laptop to create a digital overlay of the patterns. Sophie, always the adventurer, theorized aloud about what the symbols might mean, her excitement driving the group forward.

After hours of work, Emma finally leaned back, holding up a sheet of paper covered in neat rows of interconnected symbols. "This is it," she said, her voice filled with triumph. "The sequence. It starts with the solstice spiral and moves outward."

Max examined the sequence, nodding slowly. "It's not just random. Look—these symbols line up with the star patterns I found in Ava's map. They're astronomical markers."

"And these—" Sophie pointed to a series of jagged lines "—look like the layout of Stonehenge itself."

"So it's a combination," Emma said. "Astronomical alignments and site geometry."

"But where does it lead?" Ava asked.

Emma pulled out the drone footage Leo had taken of the field. She placed the sequence over the patterns they'd discovered and traced the lines. "It leads here," she said, tapping the screen. "The center of the field. The spot where the grass was thinner."

"The foundation," Max said, his eyes widening. "That's where the sequence ends."

The siblings stared at the screen, the weight of their discovery sinking in. Stonehenge wasn't just a monument or a calendar—it was a carefully constructed map, one that pointed to something hidden beneath the earth.

"We need to go back," Sophie said, her voice filled with determination. "We have to see what's there."

Emma hesitated, her practical side warring with her curiosity. "We need to be careful. Whatever's buried there might be dangerous."

"Or amazing," Sophie countered, her grin wide.

"Or both," Ava said quietly, clutching her sketchpad.

As the siblings packed their gear for the next day, the excitement in the air was palpable. They had cracked the code, uncovering a sequence that tied the solstice, Stonehenge, and the surrounding landscape into a single, unified purpose.

But as they prepared to leave, a chill breeze swept through the room, carrying with it a faint, unexplainable whisper. For a moment, they all froze, the sense of triumph replaced by something colder.

"What was that?" Leo asked, glancing at the others.

Emma shook her head, her expression serious. "I don't know. But I think we're about to find out."

Chapter 12: Strangers in the Dark

The early evening air was cool as the Edmondson siblings made their way back from their latest excursion to the Stonehenge site. Their discovery of the sequence tied to the solstice had electrified them, but it also left them feeling exposed. Each of them felt it in their own way: the prickling sensation of being watched.

"Are you sure we're not just imagining it?" Sophie asked, glancing over her shoulder for the third time in five minutes. The narrow dirt path they were following wound through a small wooded area near their hotel, and the shadows seemed to stretch longer than they should.

"We're not imagining anything," Emma said firmly. "I saw them too."

"Who?" Ava asked, clutching her sketchpad tightly to her chest.

"I don't know," Emma admitted. "But I caught someone watching us at the visitor center earlier. They were trying to look casual, but it was obvious."

"I saw someone too," Max added, his voice low. "By the stone field when we were packing up. They were standing near the fence, just... staring."

Leo snorted nervously. "Well, that's not creepy at all."

As they rounded a bend in the path, the group slowed, their ears straining against the rustling leaves and distant hum of traffic. Emma stopped abruptly, holding up a hand. The others froze.

"Do you hear that?" she whispered.

The siblings listened. At first, it was faint—a soft crunch of footsteps on gravel, too far behind them to be their own. The sound grew louder for a moment, then stopped.

"Someone's following us," Sophie whispered, her excitement laced with unease.

"Don't panic," Emma said, her voice steady. "Keep walking, but stay close."

They picked up their pace, their footsteps quick and purposeful. The path was narrow, bordered by tall hedges and scattered trees, offering few places to hide if they were confronted. The footsteps behind them resumed, faster now, as though whoever was following had realized they'd been noticed.

"I'm going to look," Sophie whispered, veering slightly to the side.

"No!" Emma hissed, grabbing her arm. "Stay together."

But Sophie's curiosity had already taken over. Before anyone could stop her, she darted behind a tree, crouching low and peering back down the path. Her heart raced as she scanned the shadows, her breath catching when she finally saw them.

Two figures, dressed in dark clothing, were moving quickly and quietly along the path. They weren't talking, and their faces were obscured by the dim light. Sophie's stomach churned as one of them stopped, crouching low and scanning the area, as if searching for something—or someone.

Sophie ducked lower, her pulse hammering in her ears. She wanted to move, to run back to her siblings, but fear rooted her to the spot.

Meanwhile, Emma and the others had realized Sophie was no longer with them.

"Where is she?" Ava asked, her voice panicked.

"She's gone ahead," Emma said, her jaw tightening. "Or stayed behind."

"Should we go back?" Max asked.

"No," Emma said. "We don't know who's back there."

"What if they find her?" Leo asked, his face pale.

"They won't," Emma said, though the words felt hollow. "She's smart."

At that moment, Sophie appeared out of the shadows, her face pale and her breath short. "We need to move. Now."

Emma grabbed her arm, pulling her back into the group. "What did you see?"

"Two of them," Sophie said, her voice shaking. "They're following us. And they're not just some random tourists."

Emma's expression hardened. "Let's go. Quick, but not too obvious."

The siblings picked up their pace, staying close together as they moved toward the edge of the wooded area. The path opened into a small clearing near their hotel, and the bright lights of the nearby street offered a fleeting sense of security. But none of them felt safe.

That night, back in their hotel room, the siblings huddled together, their earlier excitement about the sequence replaced by a cold, creeping unease.

"Who do you think they were?" Ava asked, her voice small.

"Probably people after the same thing we are," Max said. "The artifact."

"But how do they know about it?" Sophie asked. "We only just figured it out ourselves."

"They could've been watching us for a while," Emma said. "If they saw us at the site or overheard something..."

Leo ran a hand through his hair, pacing the room. "So what do we do? Go to the police?"

"And say what?" Emma replied. "That two people were following us because we think Stonehenge is hiding an ancient artifact? They'd laugh us out of the station."

"So we keep going," Sophie said firmly. "If they're after the artifact, we have to get to it first."

"And what happens if they catch us?" Ava asked, her voice trembling.

"They won't," Emma said, though she didn't sound entirely convinced. "We'll be careful. And we'll stick together."

The room fell silent, the weight of their situation pressing down on them. For the first time, the mystery of Stonehenge felt dangerous, the thrill of discovery overshadowed by the threat of the unknown.

Later that night, as the siblings lay in their beds, unable to sleep, Emma sat by the window, her eyes scanning the street below. The faint sound of footsteps echoed in her memory, a reminder that they weren't the only ones chasing the truth.

The shadows moved outside, and for a moment, Emma thought she saw something—a figure slipping behind a parked car. Her heart raced, but when she looked again, the street was empty.

Still, she couldn't shake the feeling that the strangers in the dark were closer than they realized.

And they weren't done watching.

Chapter 13: The Relic Beneath

The morning air was thick with anticipation as the Edmondson siblings returned to the marked site in the field where Leo's drone had uncovered the faint outline of a buried structure. They had spent the night restless, their minds replaying the unsettling encounter with the strangers in the dark. But the pull of discovery was too strong to ignore. Stonehenge had one more secret to reveal, and they were determined to uncover it.

"This is it," Leo said, checking the GPS coordinates on his tablet. He pointed to the patch of grass where the thinner vegetation outlined a faint rectangle. "The underground structure should be right below here."

Emma knelt to examine the ground, brushing her fingers over the soft earth. "It lines up with the sequence we mapped. Whatever's down there, this is where the symbols were leading us."

"What do you think it is?" Ava asked, clutching her sketchpad. Her voice trembled with excitement and nervousness.

"A hidden chamber," Max said confidently. "Like the one Sophie found, but bigger. If the artifact is anywhere, it's here."

Sophie grinned. "Let's find out."

Using a portable ground-penetrating radar device from Leo's collection, the siblings scanned the area. The radar's faint beeps quickened as it passed over a section of the ground, confirming the presence of a hollow space beneath the surface.

"There's definitely something here," Leo said, his voice brimming with excitement. "It's big—at least ten feet across."

Emma examined the readings, her brow furrowed. "The entrance might be hidden. If it's anything like Sophie's chamber, we'll need to look for a weak point."

The siblings spread out, searching for any sign of an opening. Sophie, ever the daredevil, tapped at the ground with a small rock, listening for changes in the sound. Ava carefully sketched the patterns of the surrounding grass, noting the alignment of the faint lines that crisscrossed the area.

After several minutes, Max called out. "Over here! I think I found something."

They hurried to his side, where he had uncovered a section of earth that felt unusually firm. A small stone protruded from the ground, its surface weathered but clearly worked by human hands. It was an entrance stone, deliberately placed.

Sophie knelt beside it, using a crowbar from their kit to pry it loose. With a heavy groan, the stone shifted, revealing a dark, narrow shaft leading into the earth.

"Another passage," Sophie said, grinning. "Shall we?"

Emma hesitated, her practical side warring with her curiosity. "We have to be careful. If there's another trap..."

"We'll be ready," Sophie said. "I'll go first."

"Not alone," Max said firmly. "We stick together."

The passage was narrow and damp, the air thick and heavy as they crawled downward. The siblings moved carefully, their flashlights cutting through the darkness. The walls were lined with ancient stone, engraved with the same swirling patterns that had guided them here.

"This is incredible," Max whispered, running his fingers over the carvings. "It's like the builders left a trail—something only those who understood the symbols could follow."

As they reached the bottom of the passage, the tunnel opened into a vast, circular chamber. The siblings' flashlights revealed smooth stone walls etched with intricate spirals and intersecting lines. In the center of the chamber was a raised platform, much like the one Sophie had discovered before. But this one was larger, more elaborate, and clearly meant to hold something of great importance.

The platform, however, was empty.

"Where is it?" Ava asked, her voice breaking the silence. "It's supposed to be here."

Emma stepped closer, her flashlight sweeping over the platform. "There's no dust. Whatever was here was removed recently."

"Recently?" Leo asked. "How recently?"

"Within weeks, maybe days," Emma said, crouching to examine faint scuff marks around the platform. "Look at these—they're from modern tools. Someone beat us to it."

Max's heart sank. "The artifact... it's gone."

Sophie kicked at a loose rock, her frustration palpable. "Who would've taken it? And how did they even know it was here?"

"The strangers," Ava said softly, clutching her sketchpad. "They've been watching us. Maybe they were following the same clues."

"Or they were following us," Emma said grimly. "If they knew what we were looking for, they could've let us do the hard work and swooped in ahead of us."

Max studied the platform, his mind racing. "But they can't know everything. The symbols—the sequence—there's more to this than just finding the artifact. It's part of something bigger."

"What's bigger than the artifact?" Leo asked.

"The purpose of Stonehenge," Max said. "The builders didn't just hide the artifact here. They built this chamber as part of a system. If the artifact is gone, we need to figure out where it's been taken—and what it's meant to do."

As the siblings began to search the chamber for more clues, Ava's sharp eyes caught something on the wall behind the platform. "Wait—over here."

They gathered around her as she pointed to a faint engraving etched into the stone. It was a spiral surrounded by intersecting lines, much like the symbols they had already decoded. But this one was different—beneath it was a series of small, jagged marks arranged in a pattern that resembled constellations.

"It's a star map," Max said, his excitement returning. "It's pointing to a location."

"Another location?" Sophie asked. "How many places does this thing want us to go?"

Emma examined the map, her mind racing. "The artifact isn't meant to stay in one place. It's part of a larger system. The builders created this sequence to ensure that only those who truly understood its purpose could find it—and use it."

"Then we follow the map," Ava said, her voice steady. "It's the only way to figure out where they took it."

As they climbed back to the surface, the siblings were filled with a mix of frustration and determination. They had uncovered the hidden chamber, only to find it empty. But the star map etched into the wall had given them a new lead, a new piece of the puzzle.

Above ground, the sun was setting, casting long shadows across the field. The siblings stood together, their resolve stronger than ever.

"The artifact is still out there," Emma said. "And so are the people who took it. If we want to find it, we need to move fast."

"But we're not the only ones looking," Max said, glancing nervously at the horizon. "Whoever those strangers are, they're ahead of us."

"Not for long," Sophie said, her grin returning. "Let's see if they can keep up."

The siblings exchanged a determined look before heading back toward the hotel. The mystery of Stonehenge had deepened, and the stakes had never been higher.

They weren't just chasing history anymore—they were racing against time.

Chapter 14: A Modern Mystery

Back at the hotel, the Edmondson siblings gathered around Leo's laptop, the screen glowing in the dimly lit room. The atmosphere was tense, each of them still shaken by the discovery of the empty chamber beneath the fields. The artifact was gone, and for the first time, the siblings felt like they might be out of their depth.

But Leo wasn't ready to give up.

"Okay," he said, his fingers flying across the keyboard. "If someone took the artifact, they would've needed resources—tools, vehicles, maybe even permits to dig on protected land. That's not exactly easy to pull off without leaving a trail."

"You think they left digital breadcrumbs?" Max asked, leaning closer.

"Everyone leaves breadcrumbs," Leo replied with a smirk. "The trick is knowing where to look."

For the next hour, Leo scoured the internet for any signs of unusual activity around Stonehenge in the past few weeks. He sifted through local news reports, social media posts, and even obscure forums where amateur archaeologists shared their findings. Meanwhile, Emma and Max pored over their notes, trying to connect the dots between the star map in the chamber and the artifact's possible significance.

"Got something," Leo said suddenly, breaking the silence. The others leaned in as he pointed to an online auction site featuring rare historical artifacts. One listing caught their attention: 'Neolithic Stone Relic – Origin Unconfirmed.'

"That has to be it," Ava whispered, her heart racing. The listing included a grainy photo of a small, spiralled object that looked eerily similar to the carvings they had seen at Stonehenge. The description was vague, but the price tag—six figures—spoke volumes about its perceived value.

"Where's it being sold?" Emma asked.

Leo scrolled down, his brow furrowing. "It's not a public auction. It's part of a private sale hosted by someone named 'V.P. Antiquities.'"

"Who's V.P.?" Sophie asked.

"Hold on," Leo said, opening another tab and diving into a search. A few minutes later, he found what he was looking for—a private antiquities dealer named Victor Prescott. The man's name was linked to several controversies, including allegations of artifact smuggling and dealing in black-market relics.

"Victor Prescott," Leo said, pulling up a photo of the man. He was middle-aged, with slicked-back silver hair and a polished suit, the very image of wealth and ambition. "He's notorious in the artifact world. Apparently, he's got ties to some pretty shady networks."

"So, he's a thief," Sophie said bluntly.

"More like a middleman," Max corrected. "He probably didn't steal the artifact himself. But if he's selling it, he knows who did."

The siblings sat in silence, processing the revelation. If Prescott was involved, then the artifact wasn't just a historical curiosity—it was something much bigger, something people were willing to steal and sell for a fortune.

"We have to stop him," Ava said, her voice firm.

"Easier said than done," Emma replied. "Prescott's not just going to hand it over. And if he's connected to smugglers, there's no telling how dangerous he is."

"What if we find out where the auction is being held?" Sophie suggested. "If we can get in, we might be able to get the artifact back."

"And how exactly are we going to do that?" Emma asked, raising an eyebrow. "We're teenagers, not international spies."

"We don't have to be spies," Leo said, a mischievous grin spreading across his face. "We just have to be smarter than him."

Over the next few hours, the siblings worked together to track down Prescott's operations. Leo hacked into the auction site's backend system, using his tech skills to bypass security protocols. Meanwhile,

Max searched for connections between Prescott and other artifact dealers, looking for patterns in his activities.

"Got it," Leo said finally, his voice triumphant. "The auction's happening tomorrow night at a private estate about an hour from here. Prescott's hosting it himself."

"Do we have a plan?" Emma asked, crossing her arms.

"Not yet," Leo admitted. "But we've got time to figure it out."

As the siblings brainstormed, a plan began to take shape. Leo would use his tech to monitor the auction remotely, hacking into Prescott's security cameras and communication systems. Emma and Max would pose as prospective buyers, using fake credentials to gain access to the estate. Sophie and Ava, meanwhile, would act as their backup, sneaking into the estate through a side entrance to keep an eye on the artifact.

"It's risky," Emma said, frowning as they finalized the details. "But it might be our only chance to get the artifact back."

"And figure out why it's so important," Max added.

As the siblings prepared for the auction, the weight of their mission settled over them. They weren't just chasing a piece of history anymore—they were stepping into a dangerous world of smugglers and secrets, where one wrong move could cost them everything.

But they were the Edmondsons, and if anyone could pull it off, it was them.

"This isn't just about us," Emma said as they gathered their gear. "It's about protecting something bigger than all of us. If the artifact falls into the wrong hands..."

"It won't," Sophie said confidently. "Not if we get there first."

The siblings exchanged a determined look. The game had changed, and the stakes had never been higher.

Tomorrow, they weren't just solving a mystery. They were taking on an international thief.

And they weren't about to back down.

Chapter 15: The Chase Begins

The morning sun was barely peeking over the horizon as the Edmondson siblings piled into the family's rental van. They had spent the night preparing, reviewing their plan, and gathering every resource they could think of. The auction at Victor Prescott's estate was their goal, but getting there—and figuring out how to retrieve the artifact—would require more than just showing up.

"We're racing the clock," Emma said as she adjusted her seatbelt. "If we want to stop Prescott, we need to stay ahead of him. That means tracking down anything that can give us leverage."

"And keeping out of sight," Max added. "If those people from last night were working for him, we can't let them see us."

"Got it," Leo said from the driver's seat, his tablet balanced on his lap. "First stop is here." He tapped the screen, showing a map of the area. A red pin marked a small village about thirty miles from Stonehenge.

"What's there?" Ava asked, clutching her sketchpad.

"A local antique shop," Leo replied. "Prescott has a habit of scouting smaller dealers for items to resell. I found a receipt tied to his account that matches something sold there recently—a carving similar to the ones we saw in the chamber."

"Think it's connected?" Sophie asked, leaning forward.

"Only one way to find out," Leo said, starting the engine.

The drive through the English countryside was picturesque, with rolling hills and quaint villages dotting the landscape. But the siblings had little time to appreciate the view. Their minds were focused on the task ahead.

When they arrived at the shop, a small, weathered building nestled between a tea room and a post office, Emma led the way inside. The shop smelled of old books and polished wood, the shelves lined with trinkets, pottery, and dusty artifacts.

An older man behind the counter looked up as they entered. "Morning," he said, his accent thick and friendly. "Something I can help you with?"

Emma approached him with her usual confidence. "We're looking for information about a piece you sold recently. A carved stone, possibly Neolithic."

The man's eyes narrowed slightly. "And why would you be interested in that?"

"We're researchers," Max said quickly, stepping in to support Emma. "It might be connected to a project we're working on."

The man hesitated, then nodded. "Ah, yes. Sold that piece a few weeks back. It was an odd one—spirals and markings that didn't match anything I've seen before. Came from a private collection."

"Do you know who bought it?" Emma asked.

The man frowned. "I don't usually share customer information, but..." He glanced at the siblings, then sighed. "A man named Prescott. Paid a good price for it, too."

"Victor Prescott," Sophie muttered, her suspicions confirmed.

"Do you have any record of where it came from?" Max pressed.

The man scratched his head. "The seller mentioned it was found near Silbury Hill. Said there were more pieces like it in the area."

"Silbury Hill?" Ava repeated, her eyes lighting up. "That's another Neolithic site, isn't it?"

Max nodded. "It's a huge artificial mound, one of the largest in Europe. If there are artifacts there..."

"Then Prescott might be heading there next," Emma finished. "We need to move."

The siblings raced to Silbury Hill, their urgency building with every mile. Leo drove with determination, his tablet mounted on the dashboard as he monitored live maps and Prescott's online activity. Ava sat beside him, flipping through her sketchpad and tracing connections between the symbols they'd found.

"Do you think the artifact could've been part of a larger set?" Ava asked, her voice thoughtful.

"Maybe," Max replied from the backseat. "The spirals and alignments suggest a system. If Prescott knows that, he'll be after every piece he can find."

When they arrived, Silbury Hill loomed before them, its massive, grass-covered slopes rising sharply against the sky. The area was quiet, with only a few visitors wandering the nearby paths. The siblings spread out, scanning the site for anything unusual.

"Over here," Sophie called, waving them over to a small excavation pit near the base of the hill. A tarp covered part of the area, and scattered tools suggested recent activity.

Max knelt by the edge, examining the markings in the soil. "These trenches match the ones near Stonehenge. Someone's been digging for artifacts."

Emma glanced around, her eyes narrowing. "Prescott's people might still be here. We need to move fast."

Leo activated his drone, sending it into the air to scan the area. The live feed showed a few parked vehicles hidden behind a nearby hill, along with several figures moving purposefully toward the excavation site.

"We've got company," Leo said, his voice tense.

The siblings ducked behind a cluster of bushes as the strangers approached. Ava clutched her sketchpad tightly, her mind racing as she tried to recall the star map from the chamber.

"Wait," she whispered. "I remember something. The map—it didn't just show Stonehenge. It pointed to a series of locations, like a trail."

"Silbury Hill could be the next marker," Max said, his excitement mounting. "But if Prescott's people are here, they might already have what they're looking for."

"Or they're still looking," Emma said. "Either way, we need to figure out what they've found before they take it."

Leo handed Ava his tablet. "Here—use the drone feed to mark anything that looks important. I'll handle the tech if they try to block our signal."

"Got it," Ava said, her hands steady despite the tension.

As Ava directed the drone, the feed revealed a small, glinting object partially buried in the excavation pit. Max leaned in closer. "That could be part of the artifact—or something related to it."

"Then let's grab it before they do," Sophie said, already moving toward the pit.

Emma caught her arm. "Not so fast. If they see us..."

"We'll distract them," Leo said, a mischievous grin spreading across his face. "Give me a minute to set something up."

Using his laptop, Leo hacked into the strangers' communication devices, creating static interference that drew their attention away from the pit. While they scrambled to fix their gear, Sophie and Max darted toward the excavation site. Max retrieved the glinting object—a small stone fragment etched with spirals—while Sophie kept watch.

"Hurry up," Sophie hissed as the strangers began to regroup.

"Got it," Max whispered, tucking the fragment into his bag.

They raced back to the others just as the strangers noticed them. Shouts rang out, and the siblings bolted for the van, adrenaline driving their every step. Leo gunned the engine as they piled inside, the van speeding away before the strangers could follow.

As the siblings caught their breath, Max pulled out the stone fragment, holding it up for everyone to see. The spirals were faint but unmistakable, matching the symbols they had seen in the chamber.

"It's another piece," Ava said, her voice filled with wonder. "But it's not the artifact."

"It's a clue," Emma said firmly. "And if Prescott's people are chasing it, then we're on the right track."

The van sped through the countryside, the siblings' determination stronger than ever. They had uncovered another piece of the puzzle, but the race was far from over.

The artifact was still out there, and they weren't about to let Prescott take it.

Chapter 16: Clues in the Carvings

The Edmondson siblings returned to their hotel room after another long day of chasing leads. While the others debated their next move, Max sat at the desk, flipping through the pages of his notebook. His mind buzzed with questions about the spirals and symbols they had encountered, their meanings tantalizingly out of reach. He knew the answer had to be somewhere—hidden in the ancient carvings they'd documented at Stonehenge and the fragments they'd found in the field.

Max opened his laptop and began comparing his sketches to photos he'd taken during their visits. The spirals and intersecting lines looked deceptively simple, but their repetition across multiple sites couldn't be a coincidence. He needed more information, a way to place these symbols into a broader context.

"I think we need to make a stop at the museum tomorrow," he said aloud, breaking the silence.

"The museum?" Emma asked, raising an eyebrow. "What for?"

"There's an exhibit on prehistoric Britain that includes artifacts from Stonehenge and other Neolithic sites," Max explained. "I read about it when we first got here. If the carvings we've seen are part of a larger system, maybe the museum has something that connects the dots."

Emma nodded thoughtfully. "It's worth a shot. We're running out of leads as it is."

The next morning, the siblings arrived at the museum, a stately building with towering stone columns and banners advertising the Neolithic exhibit. Max led the way, his focus razor-sharp as they moved through the galleries filled with ancient tools, pottery, and ceremonial objects. He stopped abruptly in front of a glass case containing a carved stone tablet, its surface etched with familiar spirals and lines.

"This," Max said, pointing at the artifact. "It's almost identical to the carvings we saw at Stonehenge."

Ava pressed closer to the glass, her sketchpad in hand. "It matches the designs in the shadows too."

Max scanned the tablet's informational placard, reading aloud. "This is part of a ceremonial altar unearthed near Avebury. Researchers believe the carvings represent celestial alignments and seasonal cycles, but no one's been able to fully decipher them."

"What if they're more than just alignments?" Ava asked, her voice thoughtful. "What if they're instructions? Like the ones we found in the chamber?"

Max's pulse quickened as he considered the idea. "It makes sense. The carvings could've been a way to communicate something critical, something that couldn't be written in words."

Sophie, standing nearby, gestured to another display case. "Check this out. These carvings are from a completely different site, but they have the same spirals."

The siblings moved to the new case, which displayed a collection of small stone fragments recovered from a burial mound. The spirals on the fragments were similar but more weathered, their edges softened by time. Max stared at them, the connections in his mind snapping into place.

"These symbols aren't isolated," he said, his excitement growing. "They're part of a larger network. The same symbols keep showing up at different sites because they're all connected."

Emma crossed her arms, her expression thoughtful. "Connected how? What's the purpose?"

Max gestured to the carvings, his voice rising with conviction. "Think about it. Stonehenge, Avebury, Silbury Hill—they're all aligned with celestial events. What if the symbols are part of a system for tracking those alignments? Or... what if they're pointing to something hidden across these sites?"

Leo, who had been silent until now, chimed in. "Like a puzzle. Each site gives you a piece of the solution."

"Exactly," Max said. "And the artifact Prescott stole—it's the key to putting the pieces together."

Ava flipped through her sketchpad, stopping at her drawing of the shadow patterns from Stonehenge. "These carvings match the ones from the shadows. If we can decode them, maybe we can figure out where the next clue is."

The siblings spent the next hour documenting the museum's carvings, comparing them to their own sketches and notes. Max's meticulous attention to detail paid off when he noticed a specific spiral pattern repeated on multiple artifacts. The spirals were arranged in a precise sequence, with each turn intersecting lines that mirrored star constellations.

"It's a star map," Max said, his voice trembling with excitement. "These carvings aren't just decorative—they're showing us the positions of stars at specific times. If we align these patterns with modern star charts, we might be able to pinpoint a location."

"Then let's do it," Emma said, her tone decisive. "We've got everything we need."

The siblings left the museum energized, their arms full of sketches and notes. Max couldn't stop thinking about the patterns, the intricate way the symbols connected across time and space. He felt closer than ever to understanding the purpose of the carvings—and the artifact that Prescott had stolen.

As they piled into the van, Leo turned to Max. "You're really onto something, aren't you?"

Max nodded, his mind already working on the next step. "These carvings are the key to everything. If we can decode the full sequence, we'll find out where the artifact belongs—and why it's so important."

The van sped off toward their next destination, the countryside rolling past in a blur. Max stared out the window, his thoughts consumed by the ancient symbols. For the first time, he felt like they weren't just chasing history—they were uncovering a truth that had been hidden for millennia. And nothing, not even Prescott, was going to stop them.

Chapter: 17 The Artifact's Keeper

The Edmondson family sat in the dimly lit study of a centuries-old manor house, the air heavy with the scent of aged leather and oak. They were surrounded by shelves stacked with ancient tomes and artifacts, some displayed as though they were treasures, others haphazardly piled as if hiding in plain sight. Across from them sat a woman dressed in a tailored black jacket, her silver-streaked hair pulled into a tight bun. Her name was Eleanor Castille, and she claimed to be the leader of a secretive group known only as the Order of the Obsidian Circle.

"You've stumbled onto something far bigger than you realize," Castille said, her voice calm but edged with a quiet intensity. "The artifact you seek is not merely a relic of the past. It is a key—a piece of an ancient system designed to harness knowledge and power. And it was never meant to be found."

Emma leaned forward, her hands clasped tightly. "If that's true, then why was it left in a place like Stonehenge, where it was bound to be discovered eventually?"

Castille smiled faintly. "Stonehenge wasn't merely a monument. It was a vault, one of several across the world. The artifact was hidden there as a safeguard, part of a system meant to ensure that its secrets remained protected. For centuries, the Order has worked to guard these vaults and their contents, intervening only when necessary."

"Intervening how?" Leo asked, his suspicion clear. "Like letting people steal it? Because Prescott's got it now."

Castille's expression darkened. "Victor Prescott is a symptom of the very thing we were created to prevent. Greed, ambition, the desire to wield power without understanding it. If he has the artifact, then the balance we've worked to maintain is in jeopardy."

"You're not doing a great job of maintaining it," Sophie said bluntly. "He's been ahead of us this whole time."

"Because he has resources we cannot match," Castille replied. "The Order operates in the shadows, quietly and carefully. Prescott operates with no such constraints."

Max, sitting quietly with his notebook on his lap, finally spoke. "What does the artifact do? Why is it so important?"

Castille regarded him for a long moment before answering. "The artifact is believed to be part of a mechanism—a tool that aligns with celestial patterns to reveal knowledge lost to time. Knowledge of the stars, of cycles that govern life and death, perhaps even of time itself. But such power is dangerous. In the wrong hands, it could destabilize far more than just historical understanding."

Ava clutched her sketchpad tightly, her eyes wide. "So you're saying it's not just history. It's... it's something alive?"

"In a manner of speaking," Castille said. "The artifact responds to those who seek it, guiding them only if they understand its purpose. But Prescott does not seek understanding. He seeks control."

Emma's mind raced, trying to parse the implications of what they were being told. "If this Order of yours has been protecting the artifact, why didn't you stop Prescott before he took it?"

Castille sighed, leaning back in her chair. "The Order has its limits. We cannot be everywhere, nor can we act openly without risking exposure. Prescott's network runs deep, and he has made moves we did not anticipate. But now that you've uncovered the artifact's trail, you've given us an opportunity to act."

"So what?" Leo said, crossing his arms. "You want us to keep doing your job for you?"

Castille's gaze hardened. "You've already involved yourselves. Whether you like it or not, you are now part of this. The artifact has chosen you, in its own way, to continue its path."

"Chosen us?" Sophie said, her tone sceptical. "It's a chunk of rock, not some magical destiny-maker."

"Perhaps," Castille replied. "But consider this: the symbols, the alignments, the shadows you've uncovered—they have guided you, whether you intended it or not. The artifact's path is one of discovery, and it has led you here."

Emma exchanged a glance with Max, her instincts torn. Castille's words carried weight, but they also raised questions. "How do we know we can trust you?" Emma asked. "If Prescott is after the artifact for his own reasons, how do we know you're not doing the same?"

A flicker of something passed over Castille's face—pride, perhaps, or respect. "You don't," she said simply. "Trust must be earned. But know this: Prescott seeks the artifact for personal gain, to manipulate its power for his own ends. The Order seeks only to ensure that its purpose remains intact and its power unused."

"Unused?" Ava asked. "Why wouldn't you use it if it could do so much good?"

"Because power always comes at a cost," Castille said. "The artifact's potential is too great for any one person—or group—to wield responsibly. That is why it has remained hidden, scattered, and fragmented."

The room fell silent, the weight of Castille's words pressing down on the siblings. Finally, Emma stood, her jaw set with determination. "We don't have time to debate who's right or wrong. Prescott has the artifact, and if we don't stop him, none of this will matter."

Castille nodded approvingly. "Then we must act quickly. The Order has been tracking Prescott's movements. We believe he is preparing to activate the artifact at a site connected to its original purpose."

"Where?" Max asked.

"Durrington Walls," Castille replied. "An ancient settlement near Stonehenge. It was once a place of gathering, a center of activity for the people who built the monument. Prescott intends to use the site to awaken the artifact's potential."

The siblings exchanged a glance, their resolve solidifying. They might not trust the Order entirely, but they couldn't ignore the urgency of the situation.

"We'll stop him," Emma said. "But we'll do it our way."

Castille smiled faintly. "Very well. But remember—this path you've chosen is not without risk. Once you step into this world, there is no turning back."

"We're not afraid of a little risk," Sophie said with a grin.

"Then may the stones guide you," Castille said, her tone almost reverent. "And may you find the strength to see this through."

As the siblings left the manor, the weight of their mission settled over them. The artifact was more than a historical mystery now—it was a responsibility. And with Prescott's plans unfolding, they had no choice but to face the danger head-on.

Chapter 18: A Vision of the Past

The siblings returned to their hotel room after their tense meeting with Eleanor Castille, their thoughts swirling with the revelations about the Order and the artifact's significance. While the others pored over maps and notes in preparation for their next move, Sophie found herself restless. The weight of the mystery and the constant chase had left her with an itch for answers that couldn't be scratched by planning alone.

"I'm going for a walk," she announced, grabbing a flashlight and her jacket.

"Be careful," Emma warned, barely glancing up from her notebook. "And don't wander off."

"Don't worry about me," Sophie said with a grin. "I'm just stretching my legs."

She stepped into the cool evening air, the stars shining brightly overhead. The quiet countryside felt both calming and eerie, the vastness of the landscape a stark contrast to the tense urgency of their mission. As she wandered past the edge of the property, her flashlight caught the glint of something metallic sticking out of the ground.

Curious, Sophie crouched down to investigate. She brushed away the dirt to reveal a rusted hinge attached to a partially buried wooden box. With a little effort, she pried it loose and dragged it into the light. The box was old, its wood splintered and weathered by time, but the metal clasp was still intact.

"What are you hiding?" she muttered, flipping open her multitool to work on the clasp.

After a few moments of struggle, the clasp gave way, and the lid creaked open. Inside was a collection of papers, yellowed with age and bound together with a faded leather strap. On the cover was a name scrawled in elegant handwriting: Dr. Alistair Cromwell, 1862.

"A diary?" Sophie whispered, her excitement growing.

THE SHADOW OF STONEHENGE

She flipped through the pages carefully, the ink faint but legible. The entries detailed an expedition to Stonehenge in the 19th century, led by Dr. Cromwell and funded by a mysterious patron. The writing was meticulous, documenting not only the archaeological discoveries but also strange occurrences that seemed to defy explanation.

May 15th, 1862

The alignment of the stones with the rising sun was more precise than I imagined. This place is no mere monument—it is a gateway, a connection between the heavens and the earth. My patron insists that we dig beneath the central trilithon, convinced that something of great importance lies hidden. I am sceptical, but the carvings we have uncovered suggest that the ancients knew far more than we give them credit for.

June 2nd, 1862

Today we unearthed a chamber beneath the stones, its walls covered in spirals and symbols unlike anything I have ever seen. At the center was a pedestal holding what can only be described as a relic of unfathomable craftsmanship. It hums faintly, as though alive, and its surface is etched with constellations. My patron calls it "the Stone of Cycles," claiming it holds the power to unlock the mysteries of time itself.

June 10th, 1862

We have encountered resistance—locals who believe the artifact should remain buried. They speak of curses, of disasters that will follow if we disturb it. My patron dismisses their warnings, but I cannot shake the feeling that we are tampering with forces we do not understand. The relic's hum grows louder each day, and I fear what may come if it is removed from this place.

Sophie's pulse quickened as she read the final entry, the handwriting jagged and frantic.

June 15th, 1862

The artifact is gone. My patron has taken it, vanishing into the night without a word. The villagers are furious, their warnings echoing in my mind. I have sealed the chamber, hoping to keep what remains safe, but I fear it is too late. The balance has been disturbed. If the Stone of Cycles ever returns to this place, may those who seek it tread carefully, for its power is not meant for the hands of men.

Sophie stared at the pages, her heart pounding. The diary didn't just confirm the existence of the artifact—it revealed that it had been taken more than a century ago, triggering a chain of events that seemed to ripple through time. The mention of the "Stone of Cycles" sent a chill down her spine. If Prescott intended to reactivate the artifact, he might not fully understand the consequences.

She tucked the diary under her arm and hurried back to the hotel, her flashlight cutting through the dark. When she burst into the room, the others looked up in surprise.

"Sophie, what—" Emma began, but Sophie cut her off, dropping the diary onto the table.

"Look at this," she said, flipping to the relevant pages. "It's a diary from 1862. An archaeologist found the artifact at Stonehenge—he called it the 'Stone of Cycles.' And get this: it was stolen back then too."

The siblings crowded around the diary, their faces a mix of awe and apprehension as Sophie summarized the entries. Max scanned the passages intently, nodding as he absorbed the details.

"This explains so much," Max said. "The carvings, the chambers—it all connects. The artifact isn't just part of Stonehenge. It's part of something bigger, something the ancients tried to protect."

"And now it's back in play," Emma said grimly. "Prescott doesn't just want to steal history—he's about to unleash something we can't control."

"What do we do?" Ava asked, clutching her sketchpad.

Emma's expression hardened. "We stop him. If Cromwell's diary is right, the artifact has a purpose. We need to figure out what it is before Prescott does."

Sophie grinned, her earlier frustration forgotten. "Then let's finish what Cromwell started."

As the siblings dove into the diary, the weight of their mission became clearer. The artifact wasn't just a relic of the past—it was a force tied to the very fabric of time and the stars. And if they didn't stop Prescott, the consequences could be catastrophic.

Chapter 19: Shadowy Pursuers

The van sped along the narrow country road, its headlights cutting through the early evening fog. The Edmondsons had left the safety of their hotel moments after deciphering the last of Dr. Cromwell's diary entries. The urgency of their mission was clear—Prescott's plans were already in motion, and time was running out.

But they weren't alone.

Emma glanced in the side mirror, her stomach tightening as she spotted the sleek black SUV trailing them. Its presence had been unnervingly consistent for the past ten minutes, growing closer with every turn.

"They're following us," Emma said, her voice low but steady.

Leo, at the wheel, tightened his grip. "I noticed. They're not even trying to hide it."

"Who are they?" Ava asked nervously, clutching her sketchpad.

"Prescott's people," Max said, his voice grim. "They must have figured out we're onto them."

"They're not just following," Sophie said, turning to peer out the rear window. "They're closing in."

As if on cue, the SUV accelerated, its headlights flashing briefly as it drew nearer. The siblings exchanged tense glances, the unspoken fear settling over them.

"Hang on," Leo said, his voice determined. He slammed on the gas, the van lurching forward as the engine roared.

The chase intensified as the van hurtled down the winding road, its tires screeching around sharp corners. The SUV stayed close, its sleek frame built for speed and manoeuvrability, unlike their clunky rental van. The fog grew thicker, wrapping the road in a shroud of uncertainty, but Leo navigated with practiced precision, his eyes sharp and focused.

"They're gaining," Emma said, her tone clipped. She scanned the road ahead, searching for an opportunity to lose their pursuers. "We need a plan."

"Working on it," Leo replied, swerving to avoid a fallen branch.

"They're not going to stop," Max said. "We have to make them."

"What do you suggest?" Sophie asked. "Throw Ava's sketchpad at them?"

"Hey!" Ava protested.

Emma's mind raced, piecing together their options. Then she spotted it—a narrow dirt path branching off the main road, partially hidden by overgrown bushes.

"There!" she shouted. "Take that turn!"

"Are you kidding?" Leo asked. "That path looks like it hasn't been used in decades."

"Exactly," Emma said. "They won't expect it. Trust me."

Leo hesitated for a split second, then yanked the wheel, the van skidding as it veered onto the dirt path. The siblings jolted in their seats as the van bounced over uneven terrain, branches scraping against the sides.

The SUV hesitated at the fork, its headlights briefly illuminating the main road before turning sharply to follow the van. The pursuers' choice sent a chill through the siblings. These people weren't just chasing them—they were relentless.

"They're still on us!" Sophie shouted.

"Of course they are," Leo muttered, his knuckles white on the wheel. "We're not losing them on this path."

"Then we'll have to make them stop," Emma said, her voice firm. She turned to Max. "What do we have that can slow them down?"

Max rifled through their bags, pulling out a canister of road flares. "This might do it."

Emma nodded. "Good. Sophie, help him."

Sophie grinned, grabbing a flare and twisting off the cap to ignite it. The bright red glow filled the van, casting eerie shadows over their faces. "Now this is my kind of plan."

"Be careful!" Ava warned as Sophie rolled down the back window.

"Relax," Sophie said, leaning out. She held the flare high, then dropped it onto the path behind them. The flare bounced and rolled, spewing smoke and sparks in its wake.

The SUV swerved, its driver caught off guard, but it didn't stop. Sophie lit another flare, tossing it closer this time. The SUV braked hard, its tires skidding on the uneven ground.

"Not bad," Leo said, glancing in the rearview mirror. "But it's not enough."

The path narrowed as it wound deeper into the woods, the overhanging branches creating an oppressive tunnel. The van's speed slowed as the terrain grew rougher, and the SUV began to close the gap again.

"They're not giving up," Max said, his voice tense.

"Then we outsmart them," Emma said. Her eyes scanned the dark forest ahead, calculating their next move. "Leo, stop the van."

"What?" Leo asked, incredulous. "Are you serious?"

"Trust me," Emma said. "Just stop."

With a reluctant nod, Leo slammed on the brakes, bringing the van to a screeching halt. The siblings jumped out, Emma already giving orders.

"Into the trees," she said. "Now!"

The siblings scattered into the dense underbrush, their footsteps muffled by the thick layer of leaves and moss. Emma led the way, her sharp eyes scanning for a vantage point. She stopped at a fallen log, motioning for the others to crouch behind it.

"What's the plan?" Sophie whispered.

"We let them think we're still in the van," Emma said. "When they get close, we hit them where it counts."

"And by 'hit,' you mean?" Leo asked.

"Disable their vehicle," Emma replied. "Max, do you have anything that can work?"

Max rummaged through his bag, pulling out a small pouch. "I've got a magnetized EMP device. It's not powerful, but if I can get it close enough to their engine, it'll shut them down temporarily."

"Perfect," Emma said. "Sophie, you'll cover him. The rest of us will create a distraction."

The plan unfolded with precision. As the SUV pulled up to the abandoned van, its occupants—two burly men in dark jackets—stepped out cautiously, their flashlights sweeping the area.

"Where are they?" one of them muttered.

"They can't have gone far," the other replied.

Emma, crouched behind a nearby tree, signalled to Ava and Leo. Together, they threw rocks toward the far side of the path, creating a series of sharp cracks that drew the men's attention.

"There!" one of them shouted, running toward the noise.

While the men were distracted, Max crept toward the SUV, the EMP device clutched tightly in his hand. Sophie moved silently beside him, her eyes darting between the men and Max's target.

"Hurry up," Sophie whispered as Max reached the hood of the SUV.

Max pressed the device against the metal, activating it with a soft click. A faint hum filled the air as the device sent a pulse through the vehicle's electronics. The SUV's headlights flickered, and the engine sputtered before falling silent.

"Let's go," Sophie said, tugging Max's sleeve.

The siblings regrouped deeper in the woods, their breaths coming fast but triumphant.

"They won't be following us anytime soon," Emma said, a rare smile tugging at her lips.

"But they'll try again," Max said. "We need to stay ahead of them."

Emma nodded, her expression hardening. "And we will. Prescott's plans are falling apart. Let's make sure they stay that way."

As they disappeared into the darkness, the siblings knew one thing for certain: the chase wasn't over, but they weren't about to let Prescott—or his shadowy pursuers—win.

Chapter 20: A Cave of Whispers

The path was steep and narrow, descending into the dense woodlands that surrounded the edge of Salisbury Plain. The Edmondson siblings followed the map Ava had sketched from the carvings in Dr. Cromwell's diary, their footsteps crunching on the loose gravel and fallen leaves. The atmosphere was thick with tension, each step bringing them closer to the destination they had uncovered—a place cryptically referred to in the diary as "The Cave of Whispers."

The cave wasn't marked on any modern maps, and none of the locals they had questioned had even heard of it. Yet the carvings, the diary, and the artifact's strange trail all pointed to this hidden location, one tied to Stonehenge and its mysterious history.

"Are we sure we're on the right path?" Leo asked, his voice echoing slightly in the stillness.

"Positive," Ava replied, clutching her sketchpad tightly. "The map shows the entrance is just ahead."

"You better be right," Sophie muttered. "If I trip over one more root..."

"Quiet," Emma said, her voice firm. "We're close. Stay focused."

The siblings moved cautiously, their flashlights sweeping the darkened woods. The path finally levelled out and ended abruptly at the base of a limestone cliff. Vines and moss clung to the rock face, partially obscuring a jagged opening barely wide enough for a person to squeeze through.

"This is it," Max said, his excitement tempered by a tinge of unease. "The entrance to the cave."

"It doesn't look very welcoming," Leo said, peering into the darkness beyond the opening. "You sure about this?"

"We didn't come this far to turn back," Emma said. She knelt by the entrance, examining the ground. "Look at these marks. Footprints."

"They're fresh," Max said, his voice tense. "We're not the first ones here."

"Prescott's people," Ava whispered.

"Then we need to move," Emma said. "Let's go."

The siblings slipped into the cave one by one, their flashlights piercing the inky blackness. The air was cool and damp, carrying the faint scent of earth and something metallic. The walls were rough, carved by both nature and human hands, with faint traces of the same spirals and lines they had seen at Stonehenge etched into the stone.

"This place is ancient," Max said, his voice hushed. "It's not just a cave—it's a site. The carvings, the layout... it's connected to the same system as Stonehenge."

"Let's hope it doesn't have any traps," Sophie said, her voice laced with nervous humour.

The cave widened into a larger chamber, the siblings' footsteps echoing faintly as they stepped inside. The walls of the chamber were covered in carvings, the symbols glowing faintly in the light of their flashlights.

"Look at this," Ava said, her voice awed. She pointed to a large spiral that dominated the far wall, its lines intersecting with dozens of smaller symbols. "It's the same as the map. This must be where it all comes together."

Max stepped closer, running his fingers over the carvings. "These symbols—they're a timeline. They're marking events, aligning them with celestial patterns. This whole cave is like a record, a history etched into stone."

Emma's flashlight swept over the floor, stopping on a raised platform in the center of the chamber. It was circular, carved from the same stone as the walls, and bore the unmistakable grooves of an ancient mechanism.

"This must be where the artifact fits," Emma said, her tone decisive. "It's part of the system."

"But the artifact isn't here," Leo said. "Prescott has it."

"Maybe," Max said, crouching beside the platform. "But this place might still tell us what the artifact is meant to do."

As the siblings examined the chamber, a faint whispering sound began to echo through the cave. It was soft at first, like the rustle of leaves, but grew louder, taking on an almost human quality. The siblings froze, their eyes darting around the chamber.

"Did you hear that?" Ava asked, her voice trembling.

"Yeah," Sophie said, gripping her flashlight tightly. "What is it?"

"It's the wind," Emma said, though her voice lacked conviction. "Or an echo."

"No," Max said, his expression serious. "It's something else. The carvings—look." He pointed to the walls, where the faint glow of the symbols seemed to pulse slightly, in rhythm with the whispers.

"It's the cave," Ava said, her voice filled with wonder. "It's alive."

"Alive?" Leo repeated. "Or something's triggering it."

Max nodded. "The artifact. The carvings respond to its presence. If Prescott brought it here, he might have activated something."

The whispers grew louder, their tone shifting from eerie to urgent. The siblings instinctively moved closer together, their flashlights dancing over the walls.

"This is not normal," Sophie said. "We need to leave."

"No," Emma said firmly. "Not yet. We need to understand what's happening here."

Max turned back to the platform, his mind racing. "The carvings—their alignment with the platform—it's pointing to something beyond this chamber. The artifact isn't meant to stay here. It's meant to activate something bigger."

"But what?" Ava asked.

"Stonehenge," Max said, the realization dawning on him. "This cave is just a part of the system. The artifact is meant to reconnect with Stonehenge to complete the cycle."

"And Prescott's trying to control it," Emma said, her jaw tightening. "We can't let that happen."

Before they could discuss further, the whispering stopped abruptly, replaced by the unmistakable sound of footsteps echoing from the entrance. The siblings turned, their flashlights catching the glint of metal as shadowy figures emerged from the tunnel.

"Prescott's people," Emma hissed. "They're here."

"Great," Sophie muttered. "What's the plan?"

"Hide," Emma said. "Now."

The siblings scrambled to find cover among the rocks and carvings, extinguishing their flashlights as the chamber fell into darkness. The only light came from the faint glow of the carvings, casting eerie patterns on the walls.

The intruders entered the chamber cautiously, their own flashlights sweeping the space. There were three of them, their faces obscured by masks, their movements deliberate.

"They know we're here," Max whispered.

"Let them come," Emma said, her voice steely. "We're not leaving without answers."

As the figures spread out, the siblings braced themselves. The chamber seemed to hum with anticipation, as though the cave itself was aware of the confrontation.

The stage was set, the whispers of the past converging with the dangers of the present. The Edmondsons were no longer just chasing history—they were fighting to protect it.

Chapter 21: The Doorway of Time

The chamber pulsed with an eerie light, the carvings on the walls glowing faintly as though responding to an unseen force. The intruders, dressed in dark clothing and armed with flashlights, moved methodically through the cave, scanning the carvings and muttering to one another. The Edmondson siblings remained hidden behind the jagged rocks, their breath shallow, their hearts pounding in the oppressive silence.

"They're looking for something," Max whispered, his eyes fixed on the intruders.

"Obviously," Sophie muttered. "But what?"

"The artifact," Emma said, her voice low but steady. "They think it belongs here."

Ava, clutching her sketchpad, glanced at the glowing carvings. "The chamber feels... alive. Like it's waiting for something."

"Or someone," Leo added, his grip tightening on the multitool he had tucked in his pocket.

The intruders gathered near the circular platform at the center of the chamber. One of them, taller than the others, stepped forward and placed a small device on the platform. The siblings watched as the device emitted a faint hum, its light casting flickering shadows on the cave walls.

"They're trying to activate it," Max realized. "But they don't have the artifact."

"They're testing it," Emma said. "Trying to figure out how it works."

The taller figure pressed something on the device, and the carvings on the walls flared brighter for a brief moment before dimming again. A faint grinding noise echoed through the chamber, as if something deep within the cave was stirring.

"They're getting close," Ava whispered. "We can't let them activate it."

Emma nodded. "We need to stop them, but we have to be smart. If we act too soon, they'll know we're here."

"Or," Sophie said, her eyes glinting with mischief, "we make them think the cave is rejecting them."

"What are you talking about?" Leo asked.

"Look at the carvings," Sophie said, pointing to the glowing symbols. "They respond to sound and movement. If we make enough noise, we can distract them—and maybe scare them off."

Emma considered the plan, her mind racing. "It's risky, but it might work. Max, do you still have the EMP device?"

Max nodded, pulling the small device from his bag. "It won't do much damage here, but it can create a burst of interference."

"Good," Emma said. "Leo, you and Sophie cause the distraction. Max, use the EMP to knock out their device. Ava and I will figure out what's happening with the platform."

"Got it," Leo said, his face lighting up with determination. "Let's do this."

The plan unfolded with precision. Sophie and Leo crept along the edges of the chamber, using loose rocks to create sharp noises that echoed off the walls. The intruders tensed, their flashlights darting toward the sounds.

"What was that?" one of them muttered, his voice tense.

The taller figure held up a hand, signalling for silence. But the noises continued, growing louder and more erratic as Sophie and Leo worked in tandem to amplify the echoes. The carvings on the walls pulsed brighter, the light flickering in response to the increasing activity.

"Something's wrong," another intruder said, his voice laced with unease. "The carvings—they're reacting."

"It's just the vibrations," the tall figure said, though his voice betrayed a hint of doubt. "Focus on the mechanism."

Meanwhile, Max slipped closer to the platform, his movements quick and silent. He crouched beside the intruders' device and activated the EMP. A soft burst of energy rippled through the chamber, causing the device to spark and go dark.

"The mechanism's down!" one of the intruders shouted, panic creeping into his voice.

"Fall back," the tall figure commanded. "We're not prepared for this."

As the intruders began retreating, Emma and Ava stepped cautiously toward the platform. The carvings on the walls dimmed slightly, as if the cave itself were settling. Ava knelt beside the platform, tracing the grooves with her fingers.

"It's designed to move," Ava said, her voice filled with awe. "But it's locked. The carvings—their alignment—it's incomplete."

"What do you mean?" Emma asked, scanning the platform.

"It needs the solstice," Max said, joining them. "The carvings are set to align with the position of the sun at a specific moment. It's a mechanism tied to time itself."

Ava nodded. "And the artifact is the key. Without it, the mechanism can't activate fully."

"But what happens when it does?" Emma asked.

"Look," Ava said, pointing to a spiral carving on the wall. "It's a doorway."

Emma turned her flashlight to the carving, its edges glowing faintly. The spiral seemed to twist inward, its lines forming a vortex that disappeared into the stone. Around it were smaller symbols—stars, constellations, and what looked like the phases of the moon.

"It's not just a carving," Max said, his voice trembling with realization. "It's a map. The mechanism doesn't just open something here—it connects to somewhere else. Maybe another chamber. Or another time."

Emma's breath caught. "A doorway through time?"

"It's possible," Max said. "The ancients used these mechanisms to track celestial cycles, but this goes beyond that. This is... this is something we've never seen before."

The siblings stood in stunned silence, the weight of their discovery pressing down on them. The mechanism, the carvings, the artifact—all of it was tied to something far greater than they had imagined.

"We have to stop Prescott," Emma said finally, her voice firm. "If he activates this mechanism without understanding it, there's no telling what could happen."

"Then we wait for the solstice," Max said. "That's our window. If we can get the artifact before then, we might have a chance to control what happens."

Ava looked at the glowing doorway, her eyes wide with wonder and fear. "And if we can't?"

Emma's jaw tightened. "Then we make sure no one else can."

The siblings left the cave in silence, their mission clearer than ever. The solstice was coming, and with it, the chance to unlock the secrets of the mechanism—or to stop them from falling into the wrong hands.

Chapter 22: A Test of Courage

The Edmondson siblings stood in the dim glow of the cave, the ancient mechanism at the center of the chamber humming faintly with anticipation. The air was charged, as if the cave itself was alive and watching. The spiralling carvings on the walls pulsed faintly, a subtle rhythm that seemed to echo the beating of their hearts.

The siblings had come prepared to stop Prescott and his team, but the cave had other plans. The moment they stepped closer to the mechanism, the carvings flared brightly, and the chamber rumbled as if something ancient and powerful had awakened. A deep grinding noise echoed through the walls, and four smaller pathways opened in the stone, each leading into darkness.

"What just happened?" Sophie asked, her flashlight darting to the newly revealed passages.

"It's a test," Max said, his voice trembling with a mix of fear and awe. "The carvings—their alignment—they've triggered something. The mechanism isn't just about the artifact. It's testing us."

"Testing us for what?" Ava asked, clutching her sketchpad tightly.

"To see if we're worthy," Max replied, his gaze fixed on the glowing carvings. "This whole place—it's been designed to protect the mechanism. Only those who prove themselves can proceed."

Emma stepped forward, her jaw set. "Then we prove ourselves."

Each sibling instinctively felt drawn to a different pathway, as if the cave itself was guiding them. Emma hesitated, her protective instincts battling with the knowledge that they couldn't back down now.

"We stick together," she said firmly.

"We can't," Max replied, his voice steady despite the fear in his eyes. "The carvings show separate paths converging. It's part of the test. We have to trust each other."

Emma clenched her fists but nodded. "Be careful. If anything feels wrong, come back."

With that, each sibling stepped into their chosen passage, the darkness swallowing them whole.

Emma: The Strategist

Emma's path led to a narrow corridor lined with intricate carvings. The air grew colder as she moved forward, her flashlight casting long shadows on the walls. Ahead, the passage opened into a small chamber with a series of stone tiles arranged in a grid on the floor. On the far wall was a glowing carving of the spiral symbol.

She studied the tiles, her sharp mind instantly recognizing the pattern etched into them as a puzzle. The symbols on each tile corresponded to positions in the carvings she had studied earlier.

"A memory game," she murmured. "Testing my ability to plan ahead."

Emma knelt, tracing the path she had memorized from the carvings in the main chamber. Step by step, she moved across the tiles, her breath catching each time the ground beneath her creaked ominously. When she reached the final tile, the spiral on the far wall glowed brighter, and the passage ahead opened.

Max: The Scholar

Max's path was different—a wide, circular room with carvings covering every inch of the walls. At the center was a pedestal with an ancient scroll encased in glass. The carvings were familiar, but their arrangement was chaotic, as if pieces of a puzzle had been scrambled across the room.

"It's a test of knowledge," Max realized, stepping closer to the pedestal. "I have to rearrange the symbols."

Using his notebook, Max began cross-referencing the carvings with his earlier sketches. He worked quickly but methodically, shifting pieces on the walls like a giant jigsaw puzzle. The carvings began to align, forming a clear path that pointed to the scroll. When the final piece clicked into place, the scroll unfurled, revealing a star map that matched the patterns they had seen in the chamber.

"That's it," Max said, his voice trembling with relief. The star map pulsed with light, and a doorway opened, leading him forward.

Sophie: The Adventurer

Sophie's passage was narrow and steep, forcing her to climb over jagged rocks and duck beneath low-hanging stalactites. The air was damp, and the faint sound of dripping water echoed through the darkness.

The path opened into a larger space where a series of stone pillars jutted out over a chasm. Each pillar was spaced just far enough apart to require a leap of faith to cross. Sophie's heart pounded as she stepped onto the first pillar, the ground beneath her shifting slightly.

"Great," she muttered. "A jumping puzzle. Perfect for me."

Summoning her courage, Sophie leaped to the next pillar, her arms flailing for balance. The pillar wobbled but held. She grinned, her confidence growing with each successful jump. As she reached the final pillar, a bridge extended across the chasm, glowing with faint carvings.

"Piece of cake," Sophie said, running across the bridge as the passage ahead revealed itself.

Ava: The Observer

Ava's path was quieter, the walls smooth and unadorned except for faint carvings that shimmered like water. She followed the glow, her footsteps silent on the stone floor. The passage ended in a circular chamber filled with mirrors, their surfaces reflecting the glowing carvings in strange, distorted patterns.

"It's a trick," Ava said to herself, her voice barely above a whisper. "The reflections are hiding the real path."

She moved carefully, using her sketchpad to trace the carvings as they appeared in the mirrors. Each step required her to analyse the angles and align the reflections to reveal the true design. Sweat beaded on her forehead as she worked, her photographic memory guiding her through the maze of light and illusion.

When she aligned the final mirror, the carvings formed a spiral that opened the path ahead. Ava exhaled, her tension easing as she stepped into the next passage.

The Convergence

One by one, the siblings emerged into a final chamber, their paths converging around the ancient mechanism. The carvings on the walls pulsed in unison, as if recognizing their success.

"You made it," Emma said, relief flooding her voice as she hugged Ava.

"Barely," Sophie said, grinning despite her scraped knees. "But I think the cave likes us now."

Max stepped forward, examining the mechanism. "The paths weren't just tests. They were lessons. Each one showed us something about ourselves—and about the mechanism."

"What now?" Leo asked, his voice steady despite the tension.

"We wait," Emma said, her eyes fixed on the glowing carvings. "The solstice is coming. That's when the real test begins."

The siblings stood together, their resolve stronger than ever. The cave had challenged their courage, their knowledge, and their unity—and they had proven themselves worthy. Now, all that remained was the final test: protecting the mechanism from Prescott and uncovering the truth behind its power.

Chapter 23: The Heart of Stonehenge

The Edmondson siblings stood in the final chamber of the cave, their breath catching at the sight before them. The artifact—an intricate, glowing device—hovered above a pedestal in the center of the chamber. Its surface was etched with spirals and constellations that seemed to shimmer and shift as if alive. The carvings on the walls of the chamber pulsed in harmony with the artifact, casting a warm, ethereal glow.

"That's it," Max whispered, his voice filled with awe. "The artifact. The Heart of Stonehenge."

"It's beautiful," Ava murmured, clutching her sketchpad tightly as she stepped closer. "It's like it's alive."

"It's more than just a relic," Max said, his eyes glued to the artifact. "This is a device—a machine tied to celestial navigation and time. It's connected to everything we've uncovered."

Emma moved cautiously toward the pedestal, her eyes scanning the chamber for any signs of traps or hidden dangers. "Be careful," she warned. "We don't know what happens if we touch it."

"It's part of the mechanism," Max said, stepping beside her. "The carvings show it aligns with Stonehenge during the solstice. That's when its true purpose is revealed."

"But what is its purpose?" Sophie asked, her voice tinged with both excitement and unease.

Max hesitated, his gaze fixed on the spiralling lines of the artifact. "To measure time? To connect us to the stars? Maybe both. The ancients built Stonehenge to align with celestial cycles. This device could be the key to understanding how they saw the universe—and maybe how they interacted with it."

The siblings circled the artifact, its glow reflecting in their wide eyes. Leo crouched beside the pedestal, examining the faint carvings at its base.

"These symbols match the ones we saw in the chamber and on Ava's map," he said. "It's all connected—Stonehenge, the artifact, and the solstice."

"The diary called it the 'Stone of Cycles,'" Ava said, flipping through her notes. "Dr. Cromwell believed it held the power to track and even manipulate time."

"Manipulate time?" Emma repeated, her brow furrowing. "That's a dangerous idea."

"But it makes sense," Max said. "The ancients didn't just want to understand time—they wanted to use it. This artifact could have been a tool for aligning with celestial events, predicting cycles, or even unlocking knowledge hidden in those cycles."

"What happens if Prescott gets his hands on it?" Sophie asked.

"He'll use it for power," Emma said grimly. "And if he doesn't understand it, he could destabilize everything."

The siblings exchanged tense glances, the weight of their mission pressing heavily on their shoulders.

Max knelt before the pedestal, his hands hovering near the glowing artifact. "The carvings suggest it's activated by aligning with the stars and the solstice. Without the alignment, it's dormant—safe."

"Then we need to make sure it stays that way," Emma said. "The solstice is only hours away. If Prescott's team gets here…"

"We'll stop them," Sophie said firmly. "But what if we need to use it? To protect it?"

Emma hesitated, her gaze shifting to Max. "What do you think?"

Max studied the artifact, the spirals and constellations reflecting in his glasses. "I think the artifact is a tool, not a weapon. If we use it, we need to understand its purpose. Otherwise, we're no better than Prescott."

"So what do we do?" Ava asked, her voice trembling.

"We protect it," Emma said, her resolve hardening. "We keep it out of Prescott's hands until the solstice passes. Then we'll figure out how to return it to Stonehenge—or destroy it if we have to."

The siblings nodded in agreement, their determination unshaken. They had come too far to let the artifact fall into the wrong hands.

Suddenly, a faint sound echoed through the chamber—the unmistakable crunch of footsteps on stone. The siblings froze, their eyes darting to the entrance. Shadows flickered on the walls as flashlights approached.

"They're here," Leo hissed.

"Get ready," Emma said, her voice low but commanding. "We'll protect the artifact no matter what."

Max moved to the artifact, shielding it with his body as the others positioned themselves around the chamber. Sophie picked up a loose rock, her muscles tense. Ava tucked her sketchpad into her bag and stood beside Emma, her eyes wide but resolute.

The footsteps grew louder, and the intruders stepped into the light. It was Prescott himself, flanked by two of his henchmen. His sharp, calculating eyes scanned the chamber, landing on the artifact with a greedy glint.

"Well, well," Prescott said, his voice smooth and mocking. "It seems you've done all the hard work for me. How convenient."

"Stay back," Emma said, her voice strong. "You don't know what you're dealing with."

Prescott chuckled, his footsteps deliberate as he stepped closer. "Oh, but I do. This artifact is the culmination of centuries of mystery. And now, it belongs to me."

"Not if we have anything to say about it," Sophie said, stepping forward with her makeshift weapon.

Prescott's henchmen moved to block her, but Emma raised her hand, signalling for them to stop. "You don't understand," she said, her voice steady. "The artifact isn't just a relic—it's tied to forces you can't control. If you activate it without understanding its purpose, you'll unleash something none of us can stop."

Prescott smirked, unfazed. "That sounds like a risk I'm willing to take."

Max's voice rang out, firm and clear. "You can't take it. The artifact isn't meant for greed or power. It's meant to guide, to connect us to something greater. If you misuse it, you'll destroy everything it represents."

Prescott hesitated for a fraction of a second, but his expression quickly hardened. "Enough of this. Take it."

The henchmen lunged toward the artifact, but the siblings moved as one, their determination unshakable. Sophie and Leo intercepted the attackers, their quick thinking and bravery buying Max time to shield the artifact.

The chamber pulsed with energy as the siblings fought to protect the artifact. The carvings on the walls glowed brighter, the hum of the mechanism growing louder. The artifact seemed to respond to the chaos, its light intensifying as if urging them to act.

"Max!" Emma shouted. "Can you do anything?"

Max turned to the artifact, his hands trembling as he reached for it. The moment his fingers brushed its surface, the carvings on the walls flared with brilliant light, and the chamber filled with a deep, resonant hum. The artifact pulsed in his hands, its spirals aligning perfectly with the carvings around them.

"It's activating!" Max shouted, his voice barely audible over the noise.

"What does that mean?" Ava cried.

"It means we don't have much time!" Max replied.

The siblings held their ground as the artifact's power surged, its light filling the chamber with an otherworldly glow. Whatever secrets the artifact held, they were on the brink of discovery—or destruction.

Chapter 24: A Sacred Warning

The chamber's brilliance was almost blinding as the artifact pulsed in Max's hands, its spirals and constellations glowing with an intensity that seemed to transcend time. The carvings on the walls of the cave flared brighter, and the hum of the ancient mechanism reverberated through the stone, like a heartbeat growing louder and stronger.

"Max!" Emma shouted over the deafening sound. "What's happening?"

"I don't know!" Max yelled back, clutching the artifact tightly. The light from its surface shifted, the spirals rearranging themselves, revealing new engravings that had been hidden moments before.

As if responding to the chaos, the carvings on the artifact began to emit a sequence of patterns—symbols interlocking and realigning, forming what looked like a sentence in an ancient, unfamiliar script.

"It's a message!" Ava cried, her sharp eyes catching the pattern. She pulled out her sketchpad, frantically sketching the glowing symbols. "It's trying to tell us something!"

Prescott, momentarily stunned by the artifact's sudden surge of activity, barked at his henchmen. "Take it from them! Now!"

"Don't let them near it!" Emma commanded, stepping in front of Max. Sophie and Leo moved quickly to block Prescott's men, using the chamber's rocky terrain to their advantage.

Max, oblivious to the scuffle, stared at the artifact in awe. The glowing symbols seemed to imprint themselves onto his mind, their meaning unfolding in fragments, as though the artifact itself was trying to speak directly to him.

"It's a warning," Max whispered, his voice trembling. "The artifact—it's warning us."

"What kind of warning?" Emma demanded, glancing back at him.

"The symbols—" Max gestured to the artifact as the spirals shifted again, forming a new pattern. "It's saying the artifact was created to align with the stars, to track cycles of time and unlock knowledge. But if it's misused—"

A deep rumble shook the chamber, cutting him off. Dust and loose rocks fell from the ceiling, and the carvings on the walls flickered ominously.

"—it'll trigger a catastrophic imbalance," Max finished, his voice barely audible. "It's tied to the Earth, the stars, the cycles of life. If someone tries to use it for selfish purposes, it could tear everything apart."

Ava, still sketching, added, "The artifact isn't just a tool—it's a safeguard. A regulator. If Prescott activates it at the wrong time or in the wrong way, it'll break the balance it was meant to protect."

Prescott, hearing their words, paused, his expression a mix of greed and apprehension. "What kind of imbalance?" he demanded.

"Catastrophic," Max repeated, his voice firmer now. "The carvings warn of disruptions to time, the stars, even the cycles of life itself. You won't just be unlocking power—you'll be unleashing destruction."

Prescott scoffed, though a flicker of doubt crossed his face. "You're bluffing. You don't even understand the artifact's true purpose."

"We understand enough!" Emma shouted, stepping forward. "And you don't care what happens as long as you get what you want."

Prescott's eyes narrowed. "Enough of this. The artifact belongs to me."

He lunged toward Max, but Sophie intercepted him, shoving him back with all her strength. "Not today, buddy!" she shouted.

The artifact flared again, its light intensifying until it filled the chamber with a radiant glow. The carvings on the walls seemed to respond, aligning in a sequence that mirrored the spirals on the artifact. The chamber grew quiet, the hum fading into an eerie silence.

Max turned to his siblings, his face pale but resolute. "It's stabilizing itself. If we keep it here and let the solstice pass without interference, the balance will hold."

"And if it doesn't?" Leo asked, his voice taut.

"Then we'll lose everything," Max said simply.

Prescott's men hesitated, unnerved by the artifact's display of power and the siblings' determination. Prescott, however, clenched his fists, his greed outweighing his caution.

"You don't have the right to keep this from the world," he hissed. "Do you know what kind of power you're hiding? What kind of knowledge could be unlocked?"

"It's not about power!" Emma shot back. "It's about protecting the balance. If you take the artifact, you'll destroy everything it's connected to."

"Let him have it, and he'll be the last person to understand that," Sophie added, glaring at Prescott.

The cave rumbled again, more violently this time, as if responding to their conflict. The carvings flickered, and a deep, resonant tone filled the chamber—a sound that seemed to come from the artifact itself.

"It's giving us one last chance," Max said, stepping forward with the artifact. "Leave now, or we'll all face the consequences."

For a moment, Prescott hesitated. The flickering light, the rumbling earth, and the unwavering resolve of the siblings seemed to unnerve even him. His henchmen exchanged uneasy glances, clearly reconsidering their loyalty.

Prescott growled in frustration but stepped back, raising his hands. "This isn't over," he snarled. "You think you've won, but you're just delaying the inevitable."

With a nod, his men retreated, following him out of the chamber. The siblings remained still, their breaths held, until the sound of footsteps faded into the distance.

As the cave settled into silence once more, the siblings gathered around the artifact. Its glow softened, the spirals returning to their original alignment.

"What now?" Ava asked, her voice small.

"We wait," Max said, setting the artifact back on the pedestal. "The solstice is almost here. When the alignment completes, the artifact will stabilize, and we'll figure out how to protect it for good."

"And if Prescott comes back?" Sophie asked.

Emma looked at the others, her expression steely. "Then we stop him. Again."

The siblings stood together, their resolve stronger than ever. The artifact had warned them of the stakes—of the catastrophic consequences that could follow if it fell into the wrong hands. And they were determined to ensure that wouldn't happen, no matter the cost.

Chapter 25: The Solstice Mechanism

As the hours passed, the cave seemed to hold its breath, the air heavy with anticipation. The carvings on the walls pulsed faintly, their glow matching the artifact's rhythmic hum. Outside, the sky began to shift, the approaching solstice marking the celestial alignment that had guided the Edmondson siblings to this point.

Leo and Max sat cross-legged near the artifact, their tools and notebooks spread out between them. The others lingered nearby, their eyes alternating between the glowing walls and the entrance, on high alert for Prescott's return. But for Leo and Max, the outside world faded away as they worked to uncover the artifact's secrets.

"This is unlike anything we've ever seen," Max said, his voice a mix of awe and concentration. He ran his fingers over the spiralling engravings, noting how they seemed to shift and realign with the faint vibrations of the cave.

"It's not just a relic," Leo said, his brow furrowed as he examined the artifact's surface. "It's an actual mechanism, a machine. The spirals—they're not random. They're part of a complex system designed to interact with Stonehenge and the stars."

"Like a celestial compass," Max added, flipping through his notes. "It aligns with the positions of the sun, moon, and stars during specific times, tracking their movements across the sky."

"But it's more than that," Leo said, adjusting his tablet to overlay the artifact's design with the star maps they had gathered. "Look at how these spirals match the celestial patterns Ava sketched. The artifact doesn't just track—it calculates. It's mapping cosmic events across time."

The two brothers worked in perfect synchronization, their strengths complementing each other. Max delved into the historical and symbolic meanings behind the carvings, referencing ancient texts and star charts. Leo, with his knack for technology, used his tablet to model the artifact's alignment with Stonehenge.

"Here's what I think," Max said, tapping his pencil against his notebook. "The artifact is designed to interact with Stonehenge as part of a larger system. The stones act as a receiver, channelling celestial energy and focusing it into this mechanism."

"And the artifact is the key that unlocks the system," Leo added. "Without it, the alignment doesn't complete. It's like the final piece of a puzzle."

Emma stepped closer, her arms crossed. "But what happens when the puzzle is complete? What's the purpose of all this?"

Max hesitated, his eyes scanning the glowing spirals. "It's... unclear. The carvings suggest the system is meant to reveal knowledge—maybe about the stars, or the passage of time. But the warnings also suggest it could disrupt those cycles if used incorrectly."

Leo nodded. "If it aligns with Stonehenge during the solstice, it might amplify the celestial energy flowing through the site. If that energy is misdirected..."

"Catastrophe," Emma finished grimly.

Ava, who had been quietly sketching the glowing patterns, spoke up. "The spirals—they're cycles, right? What if the artifact isn't just tracking time, but connecting it? Like a bridge between different moments?"

Max's eyes widened. "That makes sense. Stonehenge was built to mark celestial events, but what if this artifact takes it further? What if it connects those events across time?"

"Time travel?" Sophie asked, raising an eyebrow. "That's a bit far-fetched, even for us."

"Not travel," Max clarified. "More like resonance. Aligning moments in time to reveal knowledge or energy that would otherwise be lost."

Leo adjusted his tablet, overlaying the artifact's carvings with a 3D model of Stonehenge. The alignment became clear—a precise configuration that matched the solstice sun's position. "If we're right, the artifact uses Stonehenge's alignment to focus celestial energy. It's not just looking at the stars—it's interacting with them."

As the solstice approached, the artifact began to glow brighter, its spirals shifting into a new configuration. The carvings on the walls pulsed in rhythm, their light casting intricate patterns across the chamber.

"It's happening," Max said, his voice filled with urgency. "The alignment is beginning."

The siblings gathered around the artifact, their eyes wide as the mechanism activated. Leo's tablet beeped with new data, the readings confirming their theory. The artifact was syncing with the stars, its spirals spinning slowly as it processed the celestial alignment.

"This is incredible," Max whispered, watching as the mechanism hummed to life. "It's a cosmic clock—a machine designed to unlock the knowledge of the universe."

"But it's also dangerous," Emma reminded him. "We don't know what happens when the alignment completes."

Leo glanced at her, his face serious. "We have to trust the artifact. It's been dormant for centuries, waiting for this moment. If we don't let it complete the alignment, we'll never understand its purpose."

Emma hesitated, her protective instincts warring with her curiosity. Finally, she nodded. "We'll let it finish. But if anything feels wrong, we shut it down."

The artifact's glow intensified, its spirals aligning perfectly with the carvings on the walls. A beam of light shot upward from the mechanism, illuminating a point on the cave ceiling. The siblings followed the light, their breath catching as it revealed a map etched into the stone—a map of the stars, overlaid with ancient symbols and pathways.

"It's showing us something," Ava said, sketching furiously. "A network of sites, connected across the world."

"Stonehenge is just one part of the system," Max realized. "There are others—places built to align with the same cycles, sharing the same purpose."

Leo's tablet beeped again, the data confirming the artifact's connection to other locations. "It's mapping the entire system. This isn't just about Stonehenge—it's about understanding how ancient civilizations connected with the cosmos."

The siblings stared at the map in awe, the scope of their discovery dawning on them. The artifact wasn't just a relic—it was a key to understanding humanity's place in the universe.

As the solstice alignment reached its peak, the artifact pulsed one final time, its light softening as the mechanism slowed. The chamber grew still, the carvings dimming to their original state.

"It's done," Max said, his voice barely above a whisper. "The mechanism has completed its cycle."

Emma stepped forward, placing a hand on Max's shoulder. "What did we unlock?"

Max looked at her, his eyes filled with wonder. "A doorway to the past—and the future."

Chapter 26: The Smugglers' Return

The hum of the artifact had barely faded, its spirals glowing faintly in the dim light of the chamber, when the siblings heard the unmistakable sound of footsteps echoing down the stone corridor. Emma's head snapped toward the entrance, her body tensing.

"They're back," she said, her voice low but sharp.

"Prescott," Max murmured, clutching the artifact closer to his chest.

Leo and Sophie moved quickly, positioning themselves defensively between Max and the approaching intruders. Ava stood frozen, her sketchpad pressed against her chest as the weight of the moment sank in.

"Stay calm," Emma whispered. "We'll handle this."

The footsteps grew louder, more deliberate, and moments later, Prescott emerged from the shadows. Flanked by four of his men, he stepped into the chamber with a smug expression, his sharp eyes immediately locking onto the artifact. The faint glow of the carvings reflected in his calculating gaze.

"Well, well," Prescott said, his voice smooth and mocking. "I should have known you'd figure it out. You're more resourceful than I gave you credit for."

Emma stepped forward, her posture rigid. "You're not getting the artifact."

Prescott chuckled, shaking his head. "You misunderstand, my dear. I'm not asking. I'm taking it."

Two of his men moved closer, but Emma held her ground, her eyes blazing with defiance. "You can try," she said, her voice steady. "But you don't know what you're dealing with."

Prescott's smirk faded slightly, replaced by a flicker of irritation. "What I'm dealing with is a group of children playing at being heroes.

You've had your fun, but this is where it ends. Hand over the artifact, and no one gets hurt."

"Not a chance," Sophie said, stepping up beside Emma. "You're not walking out of here with it."

Prescott's expression darkened, and he raised a hand, signalling his men to stop. "Let me be clear," he said, his voice cold. "You have something I want. If you don't give it to me willingly, I'll make sure you regret it."

"What do you mean?" Ava asked, her voice trembling.

Prescott gestured toward the entrance, and two more of his men appeared, dragging a bound and gagged figure into the chamber. It was Alaric, the historian who had first warned them about the artifact's dangers. His face was pale, and his eyes darted to the siblings in desperation.

"Let him go!" Max shouted, his grip on the artifact tightening.

"That depends entirely on you," Prescott said, his tone calm but menacing. "The artifact for his life. It's a simple exchange."

Emma clenched her fists, her mind racing. She could see the fear in Alaric's eyes, the unspoken plea for help. But giving Prescott the artifact would unleash a danger they couldn't control.

"You're bluffing," Leo said, his voice hard. "You need us to understand the artifact. You won't kill him."

Prescott raised an eyebrow, a cruel smile tugging at his lips. "Perhaps. But I wonder how far you're willing to test that theory."

The tension in the chamber was suffocating, the air thick with unspoken threats. Emma turned to her siblings, her mind racing for a plan. Prescott was a step ahead, but she refused to let him win.

"We need to stall," she whispered to Max. "Don't let him see you're scared."

Max nodded, though his hands trembled as he held the artifact. "What if he doesn't back down?"

"He won't," Emma said. "That's why we have to outsmart him."

Turning back to Prescott, Emma forced herself to meet his gaze. "If you take the artifact, you'll destroy everything it's connected to. The balance, the cycles, the alignment—you'll ruin it all."

"Don't lecture me," Prescott snapped. "You don't understand what this artifact represents."

"Neither do you," Emma shot back. "If you activate it without understanding its purpose, you'll trigger a catastrophe."

Prescott hesitated, his confidence faltering for a moment. "That's a risk I'm willing to take."

"You don't need to," Max said suddenly, stepping forward. "We'll help you understand it. But you have to release Alaric and leave the artifact with us."

"Max!" Emma hissed, but Max ignored her, his eyes fixed on Prescott.

"You want power, right?" Max continued. "Knowledge? That's what the artifact is about. But it won't work without us. We're the ones who figured out how to activate it. Without us, it's useless."

Prescott narrowed his eyes, considering Max's words. The room fell silent, the only sound the faint hum of the artifact.

"An interesting proposition," Prescott said slowly. "But how do I know you won't betray me the moment I let him go?"

"You don't," Emma said, stepping in. "But if you take the artifact by force, you'll lose everything. The carvings, the mechanism—it'll all collapse without the alignment. You've seen what it can do. Do you really want to risk destroying it?"

Prescott's jaw tightened, his frustration evident. His men shifted uneasily, the weight of the siblings' words sinking in.

Finally, Prescott raised his hand, signalling his men to release Alaric. The historian stumbled forward, his bindings cut, and Sophie quickly pulled him to safety.

"This isn't over," Prescott said, his voice dripping with venom. "You've won this round, but mark my words—the artifact will be mine."

He turned sharply, his men following him out of the chamber. The siblings watched in tense silence as the sound of footsteps faded into the distance.

As soon as they were alone, the siblings collapsed onto the stone floor, their adrenaline fading into exhaustion. Alaric sat beside them, his face etched with gratitude and relief.

"You were brave," he said softly. "But Prescott won't give up. He'll be back."

"We'll be ready," Emma said, her voice firm. "The artifact stays here until the solstice is over. After that, we'll figure out how to keep it safe."

Max stared at the glowing spirals, his mind still racing. "The artifact warned us about imbalance. If Prescott gets his hands on it again, he won't just destroy Stonehenge—he could disrupt everything."

"Then we don't let that happen," Leo said, his voice resolute.

The siblings exchanged a determined look. They had faced danger before, but this was different. Prescott's greed, the artifact's power, and the delicate balance of the universe itself all hung in the balance.

For now, they had bought themselves time. But they knew the fight was far from over.

Chapter 27: The Solstice Clock

The glow of the artifact had dimmed, settling into a steady, rhythmic pulse that seemed to echo the beat of the earth itself. The chamber was quiet except for the occasional soft hum from the spiralling mechanism. The Edmondson siblings sat in a circle around the artifact, their faces lit by its ethereal light. Alaric, still shaken but regaining his composure, leaned against the cave wall, watching the siblings with quiet curiosity.

"We need to talk about what just happened," Emma said, her voice steady despite the tension in the room. "Prescott wasn't here just to take the artifact for fame or curiosity. He has a plan."

"To use it," Max said, staring at the glowing spirals. "But for what?"

"Power," Emma said, her jaw tightening. "The artifact doesn't just track celestial events—it interacts with them. It's tied to time, to balance, to forces we don't fully understand. Prescott isn't interested in preserving history or unlocking knowledge. He wants to exploit its power for wealth."

"That's insane," Sophie said, pacing the chamber. "How does he even plan to do that? It's not like this thing prints money."

"No," Emma said, her tone sharp. "But it can manipulate cycles. If Prescott figures out how to control it, he could influence natural rhythms—weather patterns, tidal flows, even time itself. Imagine what someone like him could do with that kind of power."

"Floods, droughts, disasters," Max added, his voice grim. "He could threaten entire regions if it served his agenda."

Leo, who had been examining his tablet, looked up. "Or sell access to it. 'Pay me, and I'll stop the storm.' It's not just wealth—it's control."

The room fell silent as the weight of their realization sank in. The artifact wasn't just a relic or a tool for discovery—it was a weapon in the wrong hands.

Emma stood, her mind racing. "The solstice is the key," she said, turning to face the group. "The artifact interacts with Stonehenge during the alignment, and that's when it's at its most powerful. Prescott knows that, and he'll stop at nothing to use it."

"But how does he plan to control it?" Ava asked, clutching her sketchpad. "It's tied to the cycles of nature. It's not like you can just press a button and make it do what you want."

"That's why he needs the solstice," Max said. "The alignment amplifies the artifact's energy, but the carvings suggest it can be directed. If he finds the right configuration..."

"He could hijack the entire system," Emma finished.

Alaric stepped forward, his voice hesitant but firm. "There's something I haven't told you," he said, his eyes flicking to the artifact. "The Order of the Obsidian Circle—they've been tracking Prescott for years. He's made a fortune smuggling artifacts, but this is different. He's not just stealing for profit anymore. He believes the artifact is his way to ascend—financially, politically, maybe even cosmically."

"Ascend?" Sophie asked, raising an eyebrow. "Sounds like a midlife crisis."

"It's more than that," Alaric continued. "Prescott's been obsessed with the idea that ancient civilizations had access to powers we've lost—powers tied to the stars and the cycles of the earth. He thinks this artifact is the key to unlocking that power and bending it to his will."

"That explains his recklessness," Emma said. "He's blinded by his own ambition."

"And the solstice is his deadline," Max added. "If he activates the artifact during the alignment, he could destabilize everything."

"Or worse," Ava said softly. "What if he succeeds?"

Leo set down his tablet, his expression grim. "We need to stop him before he even gets to Stonehenge."

Emma nodded. "The solstice is hours away. If we can hold onto the artifact until the alignment passes, its energy will reset. Prescott won't be able to use it."

"But he'll come back for it," Sophie said. "We can't just keep playing defence. We need to outsmart him."

Emma paced the chamber, her mind racing. "The carvings mentioned balance. The artifact isn't just powerful—it's fragile. If we change its configuration, we might be able to make it useless to Prescott."

"Or we break it," Sophie said bluntly. "End this whole thing."

"No," Max said, shaking his head. "We can't destroy it. The artifact isn't evil—it's a tool. It's meant to protect balance, not disrupt it. If we destroy it, we could lose centuries of knowledge."

"We don't have time for philosophical debates," Emma said. "Our priority is keeping Prescott away from the artifact until the solstice passes. Then we figure out how to protect it permanently."

The siblings sprang into action, dividing tasks with practiced precision. Max and Leo worked together to analyse the artifact's spirals, looking for a way to temporarily disable its alignment capabilities. Ava sketched the configurations, ensuring they could retrace their steps if needed. Emma and Sophie positioned themselves near the entrance, watching for any sign of Prescott's return.

As the hours ticked by, the chamber grew quieter, the artifact's glow softening as it settled into its solstice rhythm. The siblings worked in silence, their movements careful and deliberate. The stakes had never been higher, and they knew one misstep could change everything.

Finally, Max looked up, his face pale but determined. "I think we've got it. If we adjust the artifact's spirals to this configuration—" he pointed to Ava's sketchpad "—it'll disrupt the alignment long enough to get us through the solstice."

"And Prescott won't be able to use it," Leo added. "But we'll need to reset it afterward to avoid damaging the system permanently."

Emma nodded. "Let's do it. But stay ready—Prescott won't give up easily."

The siblings gathered around the artifact, their hands trembling as they worked together to adjust its spirals. The mechanism resisted at first, its hum growing louder, but with each careful turn, the glowing carvings on its surface began to shift.

"Almost there," Max said, sweat beading on his forehead. "Just a little more."

The artifact emitted a sharp pulse of light, the spirals locking into their new configuration. The chamber rumbled softly, then fell silent, the carvings dimming to a faint glow.

"It's done," Max said, exhaling shakily. "The artifact is out of alignment. Prescott won't be able to use it."

"For now," Emma said, her voice firm. "But we still have to protect it until the solstice ends."

As they prepared for what they knew would be Prescott's final attempt, the siblings felt the weight of their mission more than ever. The artifact's power was undeniable, but so was the danger it posed in the wrong hands. Together, they vowed to see it through—no matter the cost.

Chapter 28: A High-Stakes Stand-Off

The hum of the artifact's disrupted alignment still resonated faintly in the chamber as the Edmondson siblings finalized their plan. They had hours, maybe less, before Prescott returned. The solstice alignment was imminent, and they knew Prescott would stop at nothing to reclaim the artifact.

"We can't keep running," Emma said, her voice steady but grim. "This ends here."

"Agreed," Leo said, his tone sharp. "But if Prescott's bringing his entire crew, how do we stop them?"

"We turn their own greed against them," Emma replied. "If Prescott wants the artifact so badly, let's make him think he's getting it—on our terms."

The siblings leaned in as Emma laid out her plan. They would set a trap using the artifact itself as bait, exploiting Prescott's desperation to gain the upper hand. With Ava's keen observational skills, Leo's tech expertise, Max's knowledge of the artifact, Sophie's agility, and Emma's strategic mind, they had a chance to outsmart the smugglers.

"It's risky," Max said, glancing at the artifact. "If anything goes wrong—"

"Nothing will," Emma said firmly. "We've come too far to let Prescott win now."

The first step was setting the stage. The siblings carefully moved the artifact to a smaller, adjoining chamber with low ceilings and limited exits, ensuring Prescott and his men would be forced into close quarters. Ava worked quickly to replicate the artifact's glow with a combination of glow sticks and reflective tape, creating a decoy that would draw Prescott's attention.

"This should hold long enough to distract them," Ava said, stepping back to admire her work.

While Ava crafted the decoy, Leo rigged a series of small devices around the chamber—makeshift sound emitters and flash triggers designed to create confusion and disorient Prescott's team.

"These won't take them out," Leo said, tightening a wire. "But they'll buy us time to move."

Max and Sophie prepared the real artifact, carefully tucking it into a secure pack and concealing it in the larger chamber. If the plan worked, Prescott wouldn't realize he'd been duped until it was too late.

"We'll keep the artifact safe no matter what," Max said, his voice resolute.

The siblings took their positions as the rumble of footsteps echoed down the passage. Emma and Sophie crouched in the shadows near the decoy chamber, ready to spring their trap. Max stayed hidden in the main chamber, guarding the real artifact, while Leo and Ava stationed themselves near the entrance to monitor Prescott's approach.

The footsteps grew louder, and Prescott's voice rang out, sharp and commanding. "Spread out! Find them, and find the artifact!"

Emma signalled to the others, her heart pounding. The trap was set.

Prescott and his men entered the decoy chamber cautiously, their flashlights cutting through the darkness. The glowing decoy artifact sat on a pedestal in the center of the room, its light flickering faintly. Prescott's eyes lit up with triumph as he approached it.

"There it is," he said, his voice dripping with greed. "Finally."

As he reached for the decoy, Leo activated the sound emitters. A high-pitched whine filled the chamber, followed by bursts of flashing light. Prescott and his men staggered, disoriented by the sudden assault on their senses.

"Now!" Emma shouted.

Sophie darted from the shadows, kicking a flashlight out of one man's hand before ducking behind a pillar. Emma grabbed a loose rock and hurled it toward the entrance, creating a sharp crack that drew the smugglers' attention away from the decoy.

"What's happening?" one of Prescott's men shouted, his voice panicked.

"It's a trap!" Prescott bellowed. "Find them!"

The chamber erupted into chaos as the siblings moved with precision, exploiting the confusion. Sophie darted between pillars, drawing the smugglers away from the decoy while Leo triggered another round of flashes. Ava slipped into the chamber unnoticed, using her quick hands to disable one of Prescott's remaining devices.

Meanwhile, Emma confronted Prescott directly, stepping into the dim light with her chin held high. "It's over, Prescott. You're not getting the artifact."

Prescott sneered, his composure cracking. "You think you can outsmart me? You're children."

"We've done it before," Emma said, her voice cold. "And we'll do it again."

As Prescott lunged toward Emma, Sophie intercepted him, sliding into his path and tripping him with a swift kick. Prescott hit the ground hard, cursing as he scrambled to his feet. Before he could regain his footing, the sound of heavy boots echoed through the cave.

It was Alaric, leading a group of local authorities who had followed the siblings' earlier tip-off about the smugglers' activities. Prescott froze, his face contorting with rage as the officers entered the chamber.

"Victor Prescott," one of the officers said, stepping forward. "You're under arrest for artifact smuggling and trespassing on protected heritage sites."

Prescott's men dropped their weapons, their defiance crumbling under the weight of the authorities' presence. Emma watched as Prescott's bravado evaporated, replaced by cold fury.

"This isn't over," he snarled, his voice low and venomous. "You've made an enemy you won't live to regret."

"We'll take our chances," Emma said, her eyes blazing.

As the authorities secured Prescott and his men, the siblings regrouped in the main chamber. Max carefully retrieved the real artifact, cradling it in his hands as the pulsing glow steadied.

"We did it," Sophie said, grinning despite her bruised knees. "We actually did it."

"For now," Emma said, her voice steady but tired. "Prescott's out of the picture, but the artifact is still dangerous. We need to make sure it's protected—for good."

Alaric stepped forward, his expression filled with gratitude and determination. "The Order will help. Together, we'll ensure the artifact is hidden where no one can misuse it."

Emma nodded, her resolve firm. "It's not just about hiding it. It's about understanding it. This artifact is a part of history, but it's also a warning. We have to respect that."

The siblings exchanged a look, their bond stronger than ever. They had faced danger, outsmarted greed, and protected a piece of history that held the key to humanity's connection with the stars.

As the artifact pulsed gently in Max's hands, the faint glow of its spirals seemed to whisper a promise: the balance would hold—for now.

Chapter 29: Shadows of Betrayal

The rush of victory after thwarting Prescott's plan still lingered as the Edmondsons and Alaric made their way out of the cave. The artifact, now carefully secured in Max's pack, pulsed faintly, its spirals dimmed but steady. The siblings were tired but determined, their focus shifting to the next step: ensuring the artifact's safety and keeping it out of dangerous hands forever.

As they emerged into the cool night air, the stars above were bright and unyielding, the solstice nearing its peak. Emma took a deep breath, her senses on high alert. They had won the battle, but the war for the artifact wasn't over.

"We need to get this to a safe place," she said, her voice firm. "The Order can help us protect it."

Alaric nodded, his expression grim. "There's a facility nearby where it can be secured temporarily. The Order has connections that—"

The sudden crack of a twig snapped everyone's attention to the woods surrounding the cave. Emma raised a hand to silence the group, her eyes narrowing as she scanned the shadows.

"Who's there?" she called, her voice steady.

The woods were silent, the stillness unnerving. Then, a familiar voice broke the tension.

"Relax," said Eleanor Castille, stepping into the clearing. The silver-haired leader of the Order of the Obsidian Circle looked calm and composed, but her sharp gaze flicked toward the pack on Max's back. "I've been following your progress. You've done well."

"Eleanor?" Max said, relief washing over his face. "What are you doing here?"

"I came to ensure the artifact's safe transfer," she replied smoothly. "You've done an incredible job protecting it, but now it's time for the Order to take over."

Emma frowned, her instincts flaring. "How did you know we'd be here?"

Eleanor smiled faintly, brushing the question aside. "The Order has eyes everywhere. We've been watching Prescott for years. When I heard he'd been arrested, I knew you'd be moving the artifact."

"Convenient timing," Sophie muttered, crossing her arms.

Emma stepped forward, her eyes locked on Eleanor's. "You've always been secretive, but this feels... different. What aren't you telling us?"

Eleanor's expression remained neutral, but there was a flicker of tension in her posture. "Emma, you've done enough. Hand over the artifact. It's the only way to ensure its safety."

"No," Emma said, her voice firm. "Not until you tell us the truth. What does the Order want with the artifact?"

Eleanor's smile vanished. "The artifact belongs to the Order. Its power is too great to be left in inexperienced hands."

Emma's heart sank as realization dawned. "You don't want to protect it—you want to control it."

Alaric stepped forward, his expression one of shock and betrayal. "Eleanor, tell me this isn't true. We're supposed to guard history, not exploit it."

"The world is changing, Alaric," Eleanor said, her tone cold. "The artifact is too powerful to be hidden away. If we control it, we can shape the future."

"No," Max said, his voice trembling with anger. "That's exactly what Prescott wanted—to use the artifact for power. You're no different."

Eleanor sighed, as though disappointed. "I was hoping you'd see reason. But if you won't give it to me willingly, I'll have to take it."

At her signal, figures emerged from the shadows, encircling the siblings. They were dressed in dark uniforms, their faces obscured, and each carried a weapon.

"Traitor," Sophie hissed, her fists clenching. "We trusted you."

Eleanor's expression softened, but only slightly. "This isn't personal. It's about the greater good."

Emma's mind raced, her heart pounding as she assessed their options. They were outnumbered and outgunned, and the artifact was too fragile to risk a direct confrontation.

"Max," Emma whispered, her voice low and urgent. "Can you disable the artifact's glow?"

Max hesitated but nodded, his hands shaking as he adjusted the spirals on the artifact. The light dimmed until it was nearly invisible.

"Good," Emma said. "Ava, stay close to me. Sophie, Leo—be ready to move."

"What's the plan?" Leo whispered.

"Stall," Emma replied. "And when I give the signal, run."

She turned back to Eleanor, her expression hardening. "If you want the artifact, you'll have to take it from us."

Eleanor's eyes narrowed. "Don't test me, Emma. You can't win this."

"Maybe not," Emma said, her voice rising. "But we can destroy it before you get your hands on it."

Eleanor flinched, her calm façade cracking for the first time. "You wouldn't."

"Try me," Emma said, stepping closer. "This artifact isn't yours to take. If you use it for your own gain, you'll destroy the balance it's meant to protect."

Eleanor's hesitation gave the siblings the opening they needed. Emma shouted, "Now!" and chaos erupted.

Sophie and Leo launched themselves at the nearest guards, using the element of surprise to knock them off balance. Ava darted toward the tree line, clutching the decoy artifact she had quickly fashioned from her supplies. Max clutched the real artifact, his grip firm despite his fear.

"Run!" Emma shouted, grabbing Alaric by the arm and pulling him toward the woods.

The guards regrouped quickly, chasing after the siblings as Eleanor shouted orders. Flashlights swept through the trees, but the siblings moved like shadows, their knowledge of the terrain giving them an edge.

Sophie used her agility to climb a low branch, kicking over a guard who passed beneath her. Leo darted behind a fallen log, triggering a flash grenade he had rigged earlier, temporarily blinding another group of pursuers.

Emma, Max, and Alaric reached a narrow stream, where Ava was waiting with the decoy artifact. "Here," Ava whispered, handing it to Emma. "They'll go after this."

Emma nodded, her mind racing. "Max, take the real artifact and keep moving. Don't stop until you're safe."

"What about you?" Max asked, his voice tight with worry.

"We'll lead them away," Emma said. "Go!"

Max hesitated but obeyed, clutching the artifact as he disappeared into the shadows. Emma, Ava, and Alaric stayed behind, planting the decoy artifact in the mud and creating a false trail.

When Eleanor and her guards caught up, their flashlights fell on the glowing decoy. Eleanor's triumphant smile returned, but it was short-lived. As she reached for the decoy, it sparked and fell apart, revealing Ava's handiwork.

Eleanor's fury was palpable as she turned to the woods. "Find them! Now!"

But by the time her guards resumed the chase, the siblings were gone, disappearing into the night with the artifact safely in Max's hands.

Reuniting a mile away, the siblings and Alaric paused to catch their breath. The betrayal still stung, but Emma's determination burned brighter than ever.

"They'll keep coming," Emma said, her voice steady. "But we'll stay ahead of them. This artifact doesn't belong to them—or anyone else. We'll find a way to protect it, together."

The siblings nodded, their bond unshaken even in the face of betrayal. The artifact's glow pulsed faintly, as if acknowledging their resolve. Together, they vanished into the shadows, ready for whatever came next.

Chapter 30: A Race Against Time

The faint hum of the artifact pulsed steadily in Max's hands, its spirals glowing dimly like an ancient heartbeat. The siblings regrouped in a hidden clearing deep within the woods, their breaths heavy and their nerves frayed after narrowly escaping Eleanor's betrayal. The solstice was at its peak, and the weight of their mission pressed down on them.

"We have to move," Emma said, her voice firm but laced with urgency. "The alignment won't last much longer. If the artifact isn't returned to its rightful place at Stonehenge, everything we've fought for could be lost."

"And if we don't make it?" Ava asked, clutching her sketchpad.

"Then the balance is disrupted," Max said, his voice grim. "The artifact's energy will destabilize, and who knows what that will unleash."

"We're not letting that happen," Leo said. "We've come too far to fail now."

Sophie tightened the straps on her backpack. "Then let's go. We've got a solstice to catch."

The siblings began their trek toward Stonehenge, navigating through dense underbrush and avoiding the main roads where Eleanor's guards might be searching for them. Every step felt like a countdown, the ticking clock of the solstice pushing them to move faster despite their exhaustion.

Max carried the artifact with reverence, its warmth a constant reminder of the power they were tasked with protecting. The spirals on its surface glowed brighter as they neared Stonehenge, as if the artifact itself knew its destination was close.

"We're getting near," Max said, glancing at the carvings on the artifact. "The alignment is already starting. We don't have much time."

The closer they got, the more obstacles they faced. The path to Stonehenge was heavily patrolled, with local authorities and Eleanor's operatives blocking the main access points. The siblings paused at the edge of a ridge overlooking the site, their eyes scanning the iconic stones bathed in the light of the setting sun.

"Look," Emma said, pointing to a group of figures near the monument. "Eleanor's already here."

"She's trying to set up her own alignment," Max said, his jaw tightening. "She doesn't have the artifact, but she's trying to force the mechanism to activate without it."

"She's going to destabilize everything," Leo said. "We have to stop her."

"But how do we get past them?" Ava asked.

Emma's mind raced, piecing together a plan. "We split up. Leo, Sophie, and I will create a distraction, draw her team away from the stones. Max and Ava, you take the artifact and get it into place. Alaric—stay with Max and Ava. Make sure the artifact gets where it needs to go."

"I won't let you down," Alaric said firmly.

Emma's team moved first, carefully descending the ridge and circling around to create noise on the far side of the site. Sophie used her agility to climb a tree and throw rocks into the clearing, sending Eleanor's operatives running toward the sound. Leo triggered a small smoke device he'd crafted, creating a haze that added to the confusion.

"It's working," Emma whispered, watching as the guards scrambled to investigate the commotion.

Meanwhile, Max, Ava, and Alaric crept toward the stones, the artifact's glow intensifying with every step. The hum grew louder, harmonizing with the faint vibrations emanating from the ancient monument.

"It's responding to the alignment," Max said, his voice filled with awe. "It knows it's home."

Ava glanced at the spirals, her fingers twitching as she sketched the glowing patterns. "It's beautiful. It's like it's alive."

As they reached the central trilithon, Max carefully placed the artifact on the pedestal where it had once rested centuries ago. The carvings on the stones surrounding them flared to life, their spirals aligning perfectly with the artifact's glow. The hum became a resonant tone, filling the air with a sound that was both ancient and otherworldly.

"It's activating," Max said, stepping back.

The artifact pulsed once, twice, and then released a beam of light that shot upward into the sky. The stars above seemed to shimmer in response, their alignment forming a constellation that mirrored the carvings on the artifact.

"It's completing the cycle," Alaric said, his voice filled with wonder. "Restoring the balance."

But the moment of triumph was short-lived. Eleanor's voice rang out behind them. "Step away from the artifact!"

The siblings turned to see Eleanor, flanked by two of her guards, a gun in her hand. Her face was calm, but her eyes burned with determination.

"You've done well," she said, stepping closer. "Now leave, and let me finish what you've started."

"No," Emma said, emerging from the haze with Sophie and Leo at her side. "You don't understand what you're dealing with. If you interfere now, you'll disrupt the balance."

Eleanor smirked. "That's a risk I'm willing to take."

The artifact pulsed again, its light flickering as the energy surged. The carvings on the stones shifted slightly, their alignment trembling as if in protest.

"You'll destroy everything," Max said, his voice rising. "The artifact is stabilizing the cycles. If you disrupt it—"

Eleanor raised her gun. "Enough! Step aside, or I'll—"

The artifact emitted a sudden, blinding flash of light, cutting her off. The hum grew deafening, the air crackling with energy. Eleanor stumbled, shielding her eyes, as the mechanism released another pulse.

"It's protecting itself," Alaric said, awe and fear mingling in his voice.

Taking advantage of the distraction, Emma signalled to the siblings. "Now! Get her away from the stones!"

Sophie darted forward, knocking the gun from Eleanor's hand with a well-placed kick. Leo grabbed one of the guards' arms, disarming him while Emma pushed Eleanor back toward the clearing. The artifact's light grew steadier, its hum softening as the siblings worked to neutralize the threat.

"You don't understand what you're doing!" Eleanor shouted, struggling against Emma's grip. "The artifact belongs to the Order!"

"It belongs to the world," Emma said firmly. "Not to you."

As the solstice alignment reached its peak, the artifact released one final burst of energy. The light filled the sky, illuminating the stones and the surrounding countryside. The carvings on the stones glowed brightly, their alignment complete.

And then, as suddenly as it had begun, the light faded. The artifact dimmed, its spirals slowing until they came to a stop. The chamber fell silent, the balance restored.

The siblings stood together, their breaths heavy, as the magnitude of what they had accomplished settled over them. Eleanor and her guards retreated, defeated but not entirely gone.

"We did it," Max said, his voice soft but triumphant.

Emma nodded, her gaze lingering on the now-dormant artifact. "For now. But we have to make sure this never happens again."

Alaric stepped forward, his expression solemn. "The Order has been compromised, but there are others who can help. Together, we'll ensure the artifact remains protected."

The siblings exchanged a look, their bond stronger than ever. They had faced betrayal, danger, and the weight of history itself—and they had prevailed.

As the first rays of the solstice sun broke over the horizon, the Edmondsons knew their journey wasn't over. But for now, the balance had been preserved, and the Heart of Stonehenge was safe once more.

Chapter 31: The Final Alignment

The siblings stood together in the heart of the monument, the artifact glowing steadily on its pedestal. Around them, the carvings on the stones pulsed faintly, their spirals seeming to breathe in rhythm with the universe itself.

"The alignment is almost complete," Max said, his voice trembling with awe. He ran his fingers over the artifact's spirals, noting how they were shifting, their patterns perfectly mirroring the rising sun's arc. "This is it. Everything the artifact is tied to—the cycles, the balance—it's all coming together."

"Then let's hope it works," Emma said, her voice steady despite the tension in her posture. "Whatever happens, we're seeing this through."

Ava crouched beside Max, sketching the artifact's glow as it intensified. "It's like it's alive," she whispered. "Like it's waiting for something."

"The solstice," Max replied. "The ancients built this mechanism to align with this exact moment. It's been dormant for centuries, waiting for the stars, the sun, and the Earth to be in perfect harmony."

"Let's hope the harmony doesn't come with a side of catastrophe," Leo said, his tone half-joking but his eyes serious.

The artifact pulsed, brighter now, its spirals spinning faster as the sunlight fully illuminated the central trilithon. A deep, resonant hum filled the air, vibrating through the stones and the ground beneath their feet.

"It's starting," Sophie said, her gaze locked on the artifact. "Everyone ready?"

"As ready as we'll ever be," Emma replied.

The hum grew louder, resonating with a power that seemed to transcend time. The carvings on the stones flared to life, their spirals glowing with a brilliant light that connected to the artifact in a network of shimmering energy. The siblings shielded their eyes as a beam of light shot upward from the artifact, piercing the sky and illuminating the constellation directly above.

"It's pointing to something," Ava said, her voice filled with wonder. "Look at the stars!"

The constellation—the same one etched into the artifact—seemed to pulse in response, its stars glowing brighter. Max's breath caught as he realized the alignment was revealing something far more profound than he had imagined.

"It's a map," Max said, his voice trembling. "A star map. But not just of the sky—it's showing a connection between Earth and… something else."

"Something else?" Sophie asked, her eyes wide. "What do you mean?"

Max pointed to the beam of light. "The artifact isn't just tracking celestial cycles. It's connecting them—bridging time and space. The ancients built this to align with cosmic events and unlock knowledge about the universe."

"But what knowledge?" Emma asked, her voice sharp with urgency.

The artifact answered.

The light from the artifact shifted, forming intricate patterns in the air around it. The patterns resolved into images—glimpses of ancient civilizations, their peoples gathered under the stars, building monuments and mechanisms similar to Stonehenge. The siblings watched in awe as the images unfolded like a story told through light.

"It's showing us the past," Ava said, her voice hushed. "How humanity worked together, guided by the stars."

The images shifted, revealing a network of ancient sites connected by glowing lines. Stonehenge, the pyramids of Egypt, Machu Picchu, and other lesser-known monuments were all part of the same system, designed to track cosmic cycles and maintain balance between Earth and the cosmos.

"This is incredible," Max said, his eyes shining. "They weren't just building monuments. They were creating a global system—a way to align with the universe and preserve balance across the planet."

"But something disrupted it," Leo said, pointing to the next set of images. The glowing network dimmed, its lines breaking apart as chaos unfolded. Natural disasters, societal collapse, and fragmentation of knowledge swept across the screen of light.

"The balance was lost," Emma said, her voice tight. "And now it's our turn to protect what's left."

The artifact's light shifted again, forming a single symbol—a glowing spiral surrounded by constellations. The carvings on the stones pulsed in sync with the symbol, and the hum reached a crescendo.

"It's giving us a choice," Max said, his voice trembling. "The artifact isn't just a tool. It's a safeguard. It's asking us to decide how to use it."

"Use it?" Sophie asked. "For what?"

"To restore the balance," Max said. "Or to destroy it."

Emma's jaw tightened as the weight of the decision settled over her. "If we activate it fully, it could realign the cycles and stabilize the system. But if we misuse it..."

"It could cause irreversible damage," Max finished.

"And if we destroy it?" Ava asked softly.

"We lose the chance to restore the system," Max said. "But we prevent anyone from ever misusing it again."

The siblings fell silent, the artifact's light casting their faces in shades of gold and silver. Emma stepped forward, her gaze steady.

"We're not destroying it," she said. "This artifact isn't just a relic. It's a reminder of what humanity is capable of when we work together. We can't throw that away."

"But how do we make sure it's safe?" Leo asked. "Eleanor, Prescott—there will always be people who want to use it for their own gain."

"We protect it," Emma said. "We hide it, and we make sure the knowledge it holds is used responsibly. Together."

Max placed his hands on the artifact, his fingers trembling as he adjusted its spirals one last time. The light intensified, the hum growing softer until it settled into a steady, resonant tone.

The siblings watched as the artifact released a final pulse of light, the carvings on the stones glowing brightly before dimming to their original state. The beam of light connecting to the stars faded, leaving the chamber in silence.

"It's done," Max said, his voice barely above a whisper. "The balance is restored."

The siblings stood together as the first rays of daylight broke over the horizon, the solstice complete. The artifact sat dormant on its pedestal, its spirals still, but its presence carried a quiet power.

"We did it," Sophie said, a tired smile breaking across her face. "We actually did it."

"For now," Emma said, her gaze sweeping the horizon. "But this is just the beginning. The balance is fragile, and it's up to us to protect it."

The siblings exchanged a determined look, their bond stronger than ever. The artifact had revealed an ancient secret about humanity's connection to the universe, and it had entrusted them with its legacy.

As they turned to leave the hallowed ground of Stonehenge, the artifact glowed faintly one last time, as if to remind them: the stars are always watching.

Chapter 32: The Guardians' Return

The solstice sun climbed higher into the sky, casting its golden light over the now-dormant artifact and the ancient stones of Stonehenge. The Edmondsons stood silently, taking in the enormity of what they had just accomplished. The artifact rested on its pedestal, its spirals still and dim, as though it had completed its purpose for now.

"We should move," Emma said finally, her voice cutting through the stillness. "Prescott might be out of the picture, but there's no guarantee he's the only one after this."

Before anyone could respond, the sound of footsteps echoed across the site. The siblings instinctively tensed, their eyes scanning the horizon. Emerging from the shadows of the outer stones were figures dressed in dark robes, their movements purposeful and calm.

"It's them," Max said, his voice low. "The Order."

Leading the group was Eleanor Castille, her silver-streaked hair catching the morning light. Her expression was unreadable, but her sharp gaze was fixed on the artifact.

"We meet again," Eleanor said, her tone as smooth as ever. "And I see you've succeeded in restoring the balance. Impressive work, though I expected no less from you."

Emma stepped forward, her posture defensive. "We don't have time for games, Eleanor. What do you want?"

Eleanor's lips curved into a faint smile. "You know what I want. The artifact must be returned to the Order, where it belongs. It's too dangerous to remain here."

"Belongs?" Sophie shot back, her eyes blazing. "The artifact doesn't belong to anyone. It's part of human history."

"And we intend to preserve that history," Eleanor replied smoothly. "But preservation requires protection, and protection requires control. You've seen what happens when it falls into the wrong hands."

"And how do we know yours are the right hands?" Leo asked.

Eleanor's gaze hardened. "You don't. But consider this: you've already done the hard work of restoring the balance. Would you undo all that by leaving it vulnerable to the next Prescott or the next reckless adventurer?"

Emma hesitated, her mind racing. She didn't trust Eleanor or the Order completely, but their resources and influence could provide the artifact with a level of protection the siblings couldn't offer alone. The weight of their journey pressed heavily on her shoulders.

Max broke the silence. "If we give it to you, we need guarantees. The artifact isn't just a tool—it's a legacy. Its purpose is to preserve balance, not to be used for power or control."

Eleanor inclined her head slightly, her expression softening. "I understand your hesitation. The Order has made mistakes in the past—allowing Prescott to slip through our fingers, for one. But our mission has always been to protect the knowledge and balance the artifact represents. I give you my word: it will be safeguarded, not exploited."

"And what if you break that word?" Emma asked, her tone sharp.

"Then the stars will judge us," Eleanor replied solemnly. "The artifact does not tolerate misuse. You've seen that yourself."

The siblings exchanged a look, unspoken questions and doubts passing between them. Ava finally stepped forward, her sketchpad clutched tightly to her chest.

"I've been drawing it," she said, her voice soft but steady. "Every pattern, every glow, every shift. We've preserved its knowledge, even if it's not with us."

Max nodded, stepping toward the artifact. "We've done our part. The solstice alignment is complete, and the balance is restored. But this artifact is too important to leave unprotected."

He placed his hands on the artifact, feeling its faint warmth one last time, and then gently lifted it from the pedestal. The Order's members stepped closer, forming a respectful semicircle around the siblings.

Eleanor extended her hands, and Max hesitated before placing the artifact in her grasp. For a moment, the glow of the spirals returned, faint but steady, as though acknowledging its new guardians.

Eleanor cradled the artifact with reverence, her expression one of solemn responsibility. "You've done something extraordinary," she said, addressing the siblings. "The balance will hold because of you."

"Just remember," Emma said, her voice firm, "it's not yours to control. It's ours to protect—for all of humanity."

Eleanor inclined her head in agreement. "And protect it we shall."

As the Order prepared to depart, Eleanor turned back to the siblings. "This isn't the end. The artifact is part of a greater system—one you've begun to uncover. Should you ever wish to continue your journey, the Order will welcome you."

"We'll think about it," Emma said, her tone guarded.

With that, the Order disappeared into the shadows of the stones, the artifact's faint glow fading with them. The siblings stood in silence, the weight of their adventure settling over them.

"What now?" Sophie asked, breaking the quiet.

Emma turned to her siblings, a small smile tugging at her lips. "Now? We go home. But this isn't the end—it's just the beginning."

As the sun rose higher into the sky, the Edmondsons left Stonehenge, their bond stronger than ever and their legacy etched into the history of the stars.

Chapter 33: A Family's Bond

The van rolled quietly along the winding countryside roads, the iconic silhouette of Stonehenge fading in the rearview mirror. The weight of their journey still clung to the siblings, each of them lost in their own thoughts. The artifact was gone, entrusted to the Order of the Obsidian Circle, but the memories of their adventure remained vivid.

Emma, sitting in the passenger seat, glanced back at her siblings. Ava had her sketchpad open, adding the finishing touches to a drawing of the artifact's final glow. Sophie leaned against the window, her scraped knees and tired eyes a testament to her daring stunts. Max was buried in his notebook, his handwriting as meticulous as ever, while Leo adjusted the settings on a drone that had seen better days.

Emma's lips curved into a small smile. "We did it," she said softly, breaking the silence.

Leo snorted. "Barely."

"But we did," Sophie said, sitting up. "And let's be real—we wouldn't have made it without each other."

Max looked up from his notebook, nodding. "We each brought something to the table. The artifact... it didn't just test our skills. It tested our bond."

"It's true," Ava said, her pencil pausing mid-sketch. "The whole time, I felt like the artifact was guiding us. Like it knew we had to work together to protect it."

Emma turned in her seat to face them, her gaze thoughtful. "So, let's talk about it. What do you think we each brought to this?"

Emma: The Strategist

"I'll go first," Sophie said, grinning. "Emma was our fearless leader. The way she stayed calm and made plans—no way we'd have survived without her."

Emma blushed slightly. "I just did what I had to. Someone had to keep us focused."

"Focused?" Leo teased. "You bossed us around."

"Which we needed," Max said, giving Emma a rare smile. "Your plans kept us alive and one step ahead of Prescott. And you always thought about the big picture."

Emma nodded, feeling a warmth in her chest. "Thanks. But I couldn't have done it alone."

Leo: The Tech Whiz

"Leo," Emma continued, turning to her brother. "Your gadgets saved us more times than I can count."

"Not to mention your traps and distractions," Sophie added. "That smoke bomb? Genius."

Leo shrugged, but a grin spread across his face. "I just like blowing stuff up."

"You don't give yourself enough credit," Max said. "Your tech helped us understand the artifact. Without your drone, we might not have found that hidden chamber."

"Okay, fine," Leo said, leaning back. "I'm awesome. But Max did the heavy lifting."

Max: The Scholar

All eyes turned to Max, who shifted uncomfortably under their gazes. "I just... pieced things together."

"Pieced things together?" Ava said, her voice incredulous. "You decoded ancient carvings, connected the artifact to Stonehenge, and figured out the solstice alignment. You were the brain behind the operation."

"And you weren't afraid to speak up when it mattered," Emma added. "Even when Eleanor tried to take the artifact."

Max nodded slowly, his expression softening. "I guess I just... trusted the artifact. And all of you."

Sophie: The Adventurer

"Okay, my turn," Sophie said, pointing at herself. "Obviously, I was the muscle. Someone had to climb, jump, and kick butt."

"Someone had to break rules," Emma said, smirking.

"Hey, it worked, didn't it?" Sophie shot back. "Besides, you needed me to get out of some tight spots."

"She's not wrong," Max admitted. "Her daring moves gave us an edge when we needed it most."

Sophie leaned back, crossing her arms with a satisfied grin. "You're welcome."

Ava: The Observer

"And Ava," Emma said, her voice softening. "You saw things the rest of us missed. Without your sketches and observations, we might never have solved the artifact's mysteries."

Ava's cheeks flushed. "I just noticed the details. You all did the hard stuff."

"Details are what made the difference," Max said. "Your sketches connected the dots between the carvings, the shadows, and the mechanism. That was huge."

"And you kept us grounded," Sophie added. "Your optimism kept me from freaking out more than once."

Together: The Edmondson Family

Emma looked around at her siblings, her heart swelling with pride. "We all brought something different to the table, but that's what made us strong. No one else could've done what we did—not Eleanor, not Prescott. Just us."

"Because we're family," Ava said, her voice filled with quiet conviction.

"Exactly," Emma said. "And that's what the artifact tested—not just our skills, but our bond. The ability to work together, even when things felt impossible."

Leo nodded, a rare seriousness in his expression. "We're a team. And we're unstoppable."

As the van rounded a bend, the siblings fell into a comfortable silence, each lost in their thoughts. The challenges they had faced—betrayal, danger, and the weight of history—had tested them in ways they could never have imagined. But through it all, they had stood together, stronger than ever.

"Where do we go from here?" Sophie asked after a while.

Emma smiled, her gaze fixed on the horizon. "Wherever the next adventure takes us."

The siblings laughed, their bond unshakable as the van carried them toward home, leaving the shadows of Stonehenge behind. The artifact was safe, the balance restored, and the Edmondson family ready for whatever came next.

Chapter 34: Echoes of Adventure

The Edmondson household had returned to a semblance of normalcy after their whirlwind adventure at Stonehenge. Max was buried in his books, Ava filled her sketchpad with drawings of spirals and stars, Leo tinkered with a new drone in the garage, Sophie was glued to a climbing documentary, and Emma divided her time between planning for the future and trying to convince herself that life might finally calm down.

But life had other plans.

It started with a letter. A weathered envelope bearing no return address arrived in the morning mail, its heavy parchment and faint scent of earth standing out among the usual pile of bills and junk mail. Emma was the first to notice it, setting her coffee mug down as she picked it up.

"What's that?" Sophie asked, peering over Emma's shoulder.

"No idea," Emma replied, flipping the envelope over. Her fingers hesitated over the wax seal, which bore an unfamiliar emblem: a stylized star encircled by spirals. "It looks... official. And old."

Max wandered into the room, already lost in thought, until his eyes landed on the letter. "Wait a second," he said, narrowing his gaze at the seal. "That symbol—it looks like the carvings we saw on the artifact."

Emma broke the seal carefully and unfolded the letter inside. The handwriting was elegant and deliberate, the ink dark against the parchment.

To the Edmondson Family,

Your recent endeavours at Stonehenge have not gone unnoticed. Your courage, intelligence, and ability to navigate the mysteries of the artifact have proven you to be worthy guardians of history's secrets.

But the artifact is only one piece of a much larger puzzle. Across the world lie other sites, other mechanisms, and other truths waiting to be uncovered. They, too, are at risk of falling into the wrong hands.

If you are willing, we invite you to continue your journey of discovery. Enclosed are coordinates to a location with ties to the artifact—a place that may hold the key to the system's true purpose.

The invitation is yours to accept—or decline. But know this: the echoes of your adventure have already reached far and wide, and the path forward will not be without challenges.

We hope to see you there.

- A Friend of the Stars

A small slip of paper fell out of the envelope as Emma finished reading. Max picked it up and studied it. "Coordinates," he said. "These lead to... the Andes Mountains."

"The Andes?" Sophie asked, her eyes lighting up. "You're telling me there's an adventure waiting in South America?"

"Looks like it," Emma said, glancing at the letter again. "But who sent this? And why?"

"It has to be someone connected to the Order," Max said. "Or someone who knows about the artifact."

"But it doesn't sound like Eleanor," Ava said, frowning. "This feels... different. Like whoever wrote it wants to help."

"Or they want to use us," Leo said, his scepticism evident. "Remember what happened with Prescott? Trusting strangers doesn't exactly have a great track record."

Emma nodded thoughtfully. "You're right. But we can't ignore this. If the artifact is connected to something bigger, we need to know what's out there."

For a moment, the siblings sat in silence, the weight of the invitation settling over them. Then Sophie broke the tension with a grin.

"So," she said, leaning forward, "are we doing this or what? Because I've already started imagining ziplining through jungle canopies."

Emma smirked despite herself. "We'll need to prepare. Research the location, figure out the risks—"

"And pack climbing gear," Sophie interrupted.

"And drones," Leo added.

"And sketchpads," Ava said quietly.

Max closed his notebook with a decisive snap. "And books. Lots of books."

Emma looked at her siblings, her heart swelling with pride and excitement. "All right," she said. "Looks like we've got another adventure on our hands."

As they began planning, the echoes of their journey at Stonehenge lingered in their minds. The mysteries they had uncovered, the bond they had forged, and the dangers they had faced had all prepared them for this next step.

The invitation promised challenges, but it also carried the thrill of discovery—and for the Edmondsons, that was reason enough to embark on the unknown.

The stars were calling again, and the Edmondson family was ready to answer.

Chapter 35: A Legacy Reborn

The Edmondson siblings were gathered around the large oak dining table, a mix of maps, notebooks, and gear strewn across its surface. The letter with its mysterious coordinates had sparked a flurry of planning and preparation, but amidst the chaos, Ava sat quietly with her sketchpad, her pencil moving in smooth, deliberate strokes.

The artifact's intricate spirals and carvings had been etched into her memory, and as she sketched, her mind returned to the glowing patterns she had seen during the solstice. The faint hum, the shifting light—it was all still vivid in her thoughts, as though the artifact had imprinted itself on her.

"Are you drawing it again?" Sophie asked, leaning over her shoulder. "Haven't you already done, like, twenty versions of that thing?"

"This is different," Ava replied, her focus unbroken. "There's something I missed before. Something in the way the spirals connect."

"Like what?" Max asked, setting down a thick book he had been poring over.

Ava hesitated, then turned the sketchpad toward him. "Look here," she said, pointing to a section of the artifact's spirals. "I didn't notice it before because the light was so bright, but I think these smaller carvings within the spirals are constellations. They're not just random—they're arranged in a sequence."

Max's eyes widened as he examined the sketch. "You're right," he said, his voice tinged with awe. "These patterns—they're star maps. But they're not just showing positions. They're... mapping movement."

"Movement?" Emma asked, leaning in. "Like tracking the stars?"

"Exactly," Max said, his excitement growing. "The artifact isn't just a clock for the solstice. It's a tool for predicting celestial events across time. These sequences could be showing how the stars shift over centuries."

Ava tapped her pencil against the paper thoughtfully. "But it's more than that. Look at the lines connecting the spirals. They don't just stop—they flow into something else. I think they're pointing to other sites."

Max flipped through his notebook, comparing Ava's sketch to his notes from Stonehenge. "It fits," he said, his voice almost a whisper. "The artifact is part of a network—a global system of sites that worked together to track and possibly influence cosmic cycles. Stonehenge was just one piece."

Leo leaned back in his chair, crossing his arms. "So you're saying there are more artifacts like this one? Connected to other places?"

"Maybe not exactly like this one," Max replied. "But there are definitely other mechanisms, other systems designed with the same purpose. If we can decode this sequence, we might be able to find them."

"And figure out what they were all meant to do," Ava added, her eyes bright with determination.

"Or stop anyone else from misusing them," Emma said, her voice firm.

As Max and Ava delved deeper into the artifact's patterns, the rest of the siblings couldn't help but watch in fascination. Max's methodical research and Ava's artistic intuition complemented each other perfectly, uncovering layers of meaning that had been hidden in plain sight.

"It's amazing," Sophie said softly. "It's like the artifact was waiting for us to figure this out."

"Or leading us," Ava said. "Every time I sketch it, I see something new. Like it's revealing itself piece by piece."

Max looked up from his notes, his face serious. "If that's true, it means we're on the right track. But it also means we're not done. Whatever this network was designed for, it wasn't meant to stay dormant forever."

The room fell silent as the weight of Max's words sank in. The siblings had always known the artifact was more than just a relic, but now its purpose felt larger, more urgent.

"We've unlocked part of its legacy," Emma said finally, her voice steady. "Now it's up to us to see it through."

"Starting with those coordinates," Leo said, gesturing to the map on the table. "If there's another piece of this system in the Andes, we need to find it before anyone else does."

"And before anyone else can misuse it," Sophie added.

Ava looked down at her sketchpad, the spirals glowing in her mind's eye. "It's not just about protecting the artifact," she said quietly. "It's about understanding it. The people who built these systems—they left this behind for a reason. Maybe it's time we figured out what that reason is."

Max nodded, his expression resolute. "And maybe it's time we uncovered the rest of the story."

The siblings exchanged a determined look, their bond stronger than ever. They had started this journey to protect history, but now they realized they were part of something much larger—a legacy that was still unfolding.

The artifact's mysteries were far from over, and the Edmondsons were ready for whatever came next.

Chapter 36: The Solstice Ends

The sun hung low on the horizon, its golden rays casting long shadows across the rolling fields of Salisbury. Stonehenge stood silhouetted against the fiery sky, its ancient stones bathed in hues of orange and red. The air was calm, filled with the quiet hum of nature and the gentle rustling of leaves.

The Edmondsons sat together on a grassy hill overlooking the monument, the weight of their journey finally lifting as the day slipped into twilight. The artifact was gone, entrusted to the Order, but its legacy—and the lessons it had imparted—remained with them.

"This is it," Max said softly, gazing at the sun. "The solstice is ending."

"And we're still standing," Sophie said with a grin, leaning back on her elbows. "That's got to count for something."

Emma smiled faintly, her gaze steady on the horizon. "It counts for a lot. We faced everything—the traps, Prescott, the Order—and we came through stronger."

"Not without a few bruises," Leo muttered, rubbing a sore spot on his arm. "But yeah, I'd say we did okay."

Ava sat cross-legged, her sketchpad balanced on her knees. She was quiet, her pencil moving in soft strokes as she captured the scene before them—the stones, the sunset, and the silhouettes of her siblings.

"You know," she said after a while, "this whole thing... it wasn't just about the artifact. It was about us."

"What do you mean?" Sophie asked, turning to her.

Ava looked up, her expression thoughtful. "The artifact wasn't just a test of skill or knowledge. It was about trust—trusting each other, trusting ourselves. We couldn't have done this if we weren't a team."

Max nodded, his eyes still on the stones. "The artifact's power wasn't just in its connection to the stars. It brought us together. Made us stronger."

"And it reminded us why we do this," Emma said, her voice steady. "It's not just about protecting history. It's about understanding it—and the lessons it has for us."

As the sun dipped lower, the first stars began to appear in the sky, their light faint but steady. The siblings sat in comfortable silence, the bond between them palpable. They had faced danger, betrayal, and the unknown, but they had done it together, and that made all the difference.

"So," Sophie said, breaking the quiet, "what now? Back to regular life? Because I've got to say, regular life feels pretty boring after this."

Emma chuckled. "For now, we rest. But we all know this isn't over. The artifact was just the beginning."

Leo smirked. "And here I thought we'd be done with all the running and danger for a while."

"Not a chance," Max said with a rare grin. "The stars have more stories to tell."

The siblings watched as the last rays of sunlight disappeared, leaving the sky awash in deep purples and blues. Ava set her sketchpad aside, leaning her head on Emma's shoulder.

"We'll be ready," Ava said softly. "Whatever comes next, we'll face it."

Emma put an arm around her youngest sister, her chest swelling with pride. "Together."

The stars above seemed to twinkle in agreement, their light eternal and unyielding. As the solstice ended, the Edmondsons knew their adventure was far from over—but for now, they had each other, and that was enough.

Chapter 37: A New Mystery Awaits

The Edmondson household had finally settled into a semblance of normalcy, or as close to it as they could manage. The siblings had returned to their routines—Max pouring over ancient texts in his room, Leo rebuilding one of his drones in the garage, Sophie testing her climbing skills at a nearby gym, Ava sketching quietly on the porch, and Emma jotting down ideas for the next big family trip.

But peace, they were learning, was fleeting.

It arrived one morning, nestled innocuously among a pile of junk mail and utility bills. The envelope was plain and unmarked, save for an ornate spiral symbol pressed into a wax seal—different from the one on the previous letter, but just as mysterious. Emma spotted it first, pulling it out with a curious frown.

"Another one?" she murmured, breaking the seal.

"What is it this time?" Sophie asked, leaning over her shoulder. "Another invitation to almost die?"

Emma didn't respond immediately. As she unfolded the thick parchment inside, her eyes scanned the neat, deliberate handwriting. The siblings, sensing the shift in energy, gathered around her.

To the Edmondsons,

Your courage and resourcefulness at Stonehenge have not gone unnoticed. The artifact you safeguarded was a vital piece of a much larger puzzle, one that has yet to be fully understood.

While you have restored balance to one part of the system, there are others—forgotten sites, hidden mechanisms, and lost knowledge—that remain vulnerable. The stakes are higher than you can imagine, and the artifact's secrets are far from fully revealed.

If you wish to continue unravelling the mystery, you will find the next piece here:

Latitude: 15.8267° S
Longitude: 70.2225° W

Proceed with caution. Not all who seek the truth do so with noble intent.

- A Watcher in the Shadows

Max grabbed his phone, typing the coordinates into a map app. "That's... Lake Titicaca," he said, his voice tinged with awe. "In South America, near the border of Peru and Bolivia."

"Lake Titicaca?" Ava repeated, her brow furrowing. "Wasn't that one of the places connected to the artifact in my sketch?"

Max nodded, flipping through his notebook until he found Ava's earlier drawings. "Yes! Look—one of the spirals aligned with a site near there. Whoever sent this letter knows about the system."

"But who sent it?" Leo asked, frowning. "The Order again? Or someone else?"

Emma studied the letter, her instincts prickling. "It doesn't feel like Eleanor. The tone is different—less controlling, more... guiding."

Sophie crossed her arms, her eyes narrowing. "Guiding us into what, though? Another trap? Or something worse?"

Emma set the letter down and looked at her siblings, her mind racing. The mystery of the artifact had always felt larger than Stonehenge, but now it was becoming undeniable. The coordinates, the cryptic warning, the references to a larger system—it was clear their journey wasn't over.

"This could be dangerous," she said finally. "We don't know who's behind this or what we'll find."

"We've handled danger before," Max said. "And this time, we're going in with more knowledge. We're ready."

Sophie grinned. "Plus, I've always wanted to see South America. Jungle treks, ancient ruins—it's basically my dream adventure."

Leo shrugged. "And I've already started upgrading my gear. Might as well put it to good use."

Ava smiled softly, closing her sketchpad. "The artifact trusted us. I think... whatever's next, it'll guide us again."

Emma exhaled, feeling the weight of the decision settle on her shoulders. They had faced betrayal, danger, and uncertainty at Stonehenge, but they had come out stronger for it. And if the artifact's secrets truly stretched across the globe, they couldn't walk away now.

"Okay," she said, her voice firm. "We'll follow the coordinates. But we do this on our terms—carefully, and together."

"Always," Sophie said, slinging an arm around her sister's shoulders.

As the siblings began preparing for their next journey, the letter lay open on the table, its words etched into their minds. The mysteries of the artifact were far from solved, and the stakes had never been higher. Somewhere in the vast expanse of the Andes, another piece of the puzzle awaited—and with it, the promise of discovery, danger, and a deeper understanding of humanity's connection to the stars.

The Edmondsons were ready for the next adventure. The stars were calling once again.

Disclaimer

This is a work of fiction. Names, characters, places, events, and incidents are either the products of the author's imagination or used in a fictitious manner only. Any resemblance to actual persons, living or dead, or actual events is purely coincidental.

While The Shadow of Stonehenge incorporates historical and archaeological elements related to Stonehenge and its cultural significance, creative liberties have been taken to craft a compelling and entertaining story. The interpretations, theories, and depictions of the monument and its history presented in this book are not intended to reflect current academic or scientific research.

Readers are encouraged to view this book as a fictional adventure inspired by the wonder and mystery of one of the world's most iconic landmarks.